"I have private information

that another expedition is going to be sent. And this is my decision. You will be on one of the rescue ships. It will be your task when you arrive on Mittend to locate the viable form of Steven Masters and release him from whatever unhappy condition you find him. His mother insists that I go personally, but that would be ridiculous. I point out to you that if your story is fact then the task I am assigning you is probably unique. You will go and rescue . . . yourself."

Certainly Steven Masters could not object to that. He had been on the first Mittend expedition and was therefore the only person on Earth with any experience of the place.

His experience, however, had consisted of returning to Earth faster than the speed of light and as another man. So back to Mittend he would go to try to unscramble the body-mind maze.

But Steven was the man with a thousand names—and only A. E. van Vogt can explain what that means in cosmic terms.

A. E. VAN VOGT

The man with a THOUSAND NAMES

DAW BOOKS, INC.
DONALD A. WOLLHEIM, PUBLISHER

1301 Avenue of the Americas
New York, N. Y.   10019

First printing, August 1974

1 2 3 4 5 6 7 8 9

Printed in U.S.A.

CHAPTER 1

★★★★★★★★★★★★★★★★★★★★★★★★★★★★

Steven Masters climbed down the ladder to the surface of the planet, wondering how he should feel. It seemed degrading that he had first to ease himself backward out of the airlock, just like an ordinary member of the crew, and then gingerly edge down the slats of the ladder.

Were films being taken? How would he look from the rear? He had a sense of moving awkwardly. He cringed with that awareness. And yet—a mixed reaction. . . . If people on Earth were really viewing this, then someone would be naming him as being the person on the ladder *at this moment*.

That possibility had its own stimulation. They're looking at me. They're seeing *me!*

His thought was: I'll go over and climb that hill, and see what this stupid place looks like.

As his feet touched the soil, Steven tried for a moment to imagine that, really, *his* contact with the new planet was the one that counted. As he had that thought, he let go of the ladder and braced himself within the frame of his spacesuit and all its paraphernalia.

Almost fell. Staggered, stumbled, fought a terrible unbalance. Good God, he was disgracing himself.

A full, perspiring minute later, he had himself braced in a leaning-back posture. And now he discovered what it was that had overbalanced him. One of the two hooks hanging down over his shoulder had caught in the handle of a canister, which had been left at the foot of the ladder. The sudden pull of the heavy object had flung him off center. Whereupon his need to keep going and the continuing weight of the object had acted one against the other, and the tough material of the spacesuit had prevented him from feeling what it was.

Steven released the hook. And stood there in such a rage that he could scarcely see.

But he realized presently that apparently none of the other crew members had noticed his wild antic.

The overstimulated feeling remained. But his anger dimmed, yielded to a partial confusion. It was a moment of stress, and an ever so tiny sliver of truth poked up through his normal condition of self-delusion. The minuscule message from somewhere inside him whispered that his aloofness during the trip had not endeared him to his fellow travelers. The realization roused in him a progression of increasing irritation that ended up as outrage. But, even so, a restraining thought remained. Better not complain.

He was walking hurriedly now in the direction of the nearest of a series of low hills. Noticing, as he approached—not volcanic. It had a steep slope, a lot of brush, mostly yellowish in color, but some green, with a hint of blue here and there. Pretty leaves, L-shaped, of all things. Nothing like that on Earth, or other discovered planets. Well (tolerantly), they did get a little education into me, in spite of all my resistance.

Yet (he couldn't help realizing) I'm already bored. The feeling: So there would be many new plants and animals. But such details really didn't matter to the son of the world's richest man.

Images of comfort flashed through his mind, as he had that thought. Fleeting pictures of fancy cars, glittering, available aircraft, well-dressed girls overly anxious to please the handsome heir. Elegant interiors, great homes, magnificent hotels, kowtowing servants—

(*"Yes,* Mr. Masters? Anything else, Mr. Masters? Shall

I bring the car out, Mr. Masters?" His own response: A shrug and a don't-bother-me attitude. "I'll call you when I need you." But if they *weren't* there: "Where the hell have you been all this time?")

On the trip to Mittend, he had discovered that there were things that money could not buy. His father's position had secured him a berth on the spaceship. It could not, once the craft was en route, take him off it, or turn it back. Such brazen use of money influence, the world did not openly tolerate.

He'd tried, by God!—and alienated everybody aboard. Not that their reactions had mattered. In certain emotional states, he was a super-communicator of negation.

Okay, so I'm bored. So you poor little creatures are looking forward to another green planet. Waiting breathlessly to see all the little birdies and the real estate. My God, it kills me just to think of spending three weeks more in space, and then a month there, and then all that endless six weeks going back.

As he strode along, bored, kind of angry, even making small movements of impatience with each step, he looked at the yellow-green world that was beginning to be slightly below him, now that he was climbing. Because the oxygen content of the air was Earth-level, he had taken his helmet off, and dropped it casually. So he could see with his naked eyes a distant forest of trees, glints of a winding river. He despised the beauty that greeted his gaze from every direction, and grimaced at the scent of the growing things around him.

A tiny, oh, ever so tiny, portion of the impatience was with himself. Steven Masters going to Mittend with the first landing party. His first expressed wish, spoken while drunk, had brought those wonderful headlines. Reading them, and the long columns about himself and his father, had done that stupid ego business. And, also, he saw now, the newspaper accounts had expanded into total purpose what had originally been a minor boastful remark at a party, and—in fact—had no purpose at all.

He mentally looked back at that asininity, pictured the dreary consequence. The conviction came suddenly: I can't survive this. It's too much.

A sense of disaster, and of how meaningless exploration really was, was like a weight upon him, as he stood finally on the crest of the hill, and gazed at all the horizons that he could see.

An odd thought-feeling passed through his mind at that instant: *"Mother, we pass on to you an image of the intruder. Have we your permission, and your power, to deal with it?"*

Steven was occasionally startled by his own stream of consciousness. But not very often, and not this time. This utterly insane meaningness flicked through his awareness, and was gone. What dominated him was irritation. There was a long ridge ahead of him, higher than all the little hills, on one of which he stood now. The ridge barred most of his view toward the, well, west.

All right, all right, he thought, resigned, I'll go over there. After all, the one thing I've always had is a kind of stubbornness. Mostly, that had been in connection with girls. It had always enraged him when some pretty little thing, instead of lying down when he pointed at the nearest bed, started the stereotyped nonsense, and made it necessary for him to grab her, and personally undress her. Whereupon, she would sigh, and relax, evidently satisfied that now it really meant something.

The way to the ridge was down into a hollow, and then up a long, shallow but jagged slope. As Steven reached the low point of the hollow, he came unexpectedly on a narrow stream, almost hidden in a shaggy, grasslike overhang. The water bubbled, and made those small sounds, and gave off a damp odor. There were little dark creatures in it. And, because he was surprised, he was, for instants only, reminded of a vacation when he was a boy, on one of his father's ranch properties—a narrow stream like this, also half-hidden, and discovered suddenly by an eight-year-old. What a joy then, what a sense of discovery, what—

His mind figuratively clamped down on that pure memory. Fifteen years of progressively more saturnine "maturity"—he called it—in instants moved massively into the time spaces between then and now.

Maturity? . . . How can you both despise being the son of a super-rich man, and take advantage of it every chance you get? Steven had worked it out easily. Have total contempt for all mankind. Take the attitude that money means nothing. Have a sneer for the old stupe, your father, for having wasted his life accumulating the worthless stuff. And, because you don't care, spend his money with a cynical profligacy.

Steven jumped the little creek, and he did two automatic positive things, then. First, he began the climb up toward the ridge, and, second, he estimated the distance to the top of the ridge at a quarter of a mile. In a way they were his two assets: to keep going forward, not just sitting, or lying down for long, or getting involved in some unchanging situation. His second asset was his locational awareness. Like a homing pigeon, he could judge directions and distances. It was not an area where he had dark thoughts, or twisted memories, or those sequential images which, in hallucinatory fashion, paraded through his mind like daytime dreams, providing him with an endless stream of fantasies by which he justified his behavior. In his time he had awakened from drunken stupors in strange beds, and yet had always known quickly where he was.

He was still striding toward the ridge, and about a hundred feet from what seemed to be a high point . . . when he saw the naked people.

"Mother, it sees us! Give us more power!"

Masters stopped. Then he did a half-twisting thing with his body. It was an unrehearsed movement, not entirely new or entirely different from anything he had ever done. There was the time he had stepped off a curb—and stepped back again with an unrehearsed rapidity, when a steam car, silent as a dark night in the country, hissed toward and then through the space where he had been a moment earlier.

In his fashion, he had been quick, then. He spun in the direction the car was going, and he registered the license number imperishably in his vindictive mind. And so began a three-year court battle, backed by the Masters money, while Steven fabricated a more and more elaborate charge against the unfortunate owner of the steam car, early getting a judgment for a million dollars, based on the totally false claim that he knew the man, and that it had been an attempt at murder. It took the Supreme Court to overthrow the judgment. That was about $84,000 in legal fees later for the belatedly successful defendant.

By then Steven believed every word of his own lies. He talked a lot after that, cynically, about how difficult it was for wealthy people to secure justice.

On several other occasions, he had responded to sudden threat with a jump, or a twist of his body, or a quick confusion of mind and muscles. Quick, because such things never lasted long for him. Even now, as he poised in awful premonition, the memories of other threats passed swiftly through his mind. And then he had the awareness that the dozen people off there to his left were not as nude as he had believed in that first look. They wore halters of some kind, which covered small portions of the mid-torso of each individual.

A second, incredibly sharp realization came. It was so sharp it hurt his insides, so intense it could be compared only to those moments of passionate hatred that he had experienced so many times in his easily offended past: the realization that this was not, *not*, NOT going to be an occasion when a court action would later win him the kind of satisfaction that always came to him when he finally got even with some—his own term—S.O.B.

Belatedly, after so many thoughts, some of them brand-new, after at least thirty seconds of half crouching and half cringing, he started hesitantly in a direction that would take him away from the strange men.

What he did was only partly running, and even then only slowly. He felt within himself a strong resistance to retreating, and a reluctance to move in the wrong direction. Almost, it was as if some barrier inside him interfered with each step. After less than a minute, when he saw that the men were not hurrying either, he slowed to a walk.

Steven continued striding rapidly but unhappily. His course was taking him roughly parallel to the ridge. Already, there was a patch of uneven ground between him and the hill over which he had originally come. And it was apparent that he would have to get back to the ship by way of a second hill, since the group of savages—he had by now noticed that they were carrying what seemed to be short spears, and so their low cultural status was obvious—could head him off if he tried going back the way he had come.

For some reason his discovery that they were in the spear-weapon stage of development made what was happening less dangerous. The whole episode seemed peaceful, somehow. Around him was a silent wilderness; the only sound, his own heavy boots, and the noise made by his spacesuit, as its various parts stroked each other. It was the suit, suddenly, that seemed to be the principal hindrance to his movements.

The moment he had that thought, he began to unscrew and unbolt, and to ease tightening levers. It was a superbly designed construction. In those final moments of undressing himself out of the spacesuit, he did have to stop, and standing first on one leg and then on the other, rid himself of the lower section.

It was as he straightened from that task, free of the awkward mass, that he saw a second group of the semi-naked people had come up from a gully less than a hundred yards away. This group also carried spears, and—also—headed toward him.

Steven broke into a run, heading now, since he was cut off from the second hill, toward the rough ground which he had been trying to avoid. He was thinking: This is ridiculous.

He came abruptly to the little creek. But it was not quite that little here, nor quite so shallow. After only a moment's hesitation, he plunged in, went down to his hips on the first step, and down to his neck on the second; and then, furious, he was climbing up a steep underwater embankment. He emerged soaking wet, sank up to his knees in mud, and then he was out of the water, and in among the rocks and other debris. Once more running.

Almost at once he stumbled and fell. Got up. Stepped into a hole and wrenched his ankle getting out. His impulse was to limp. But when he looked at his pursuers, the two groups of spearmen had somehow made better progress than he had—and were now dangerously close to inserting themselves between him and the top of the hill toward which lay whatever escape was available to him. The nearest group was only an electrifying twenty-five yards or so from him, and he could see their human faces.

It was one of those moments when time seems to stand still (but really doesn't). A moment in which everybody seems frozen in space (but only Steven actually was).

As he saw their faces unmistakably, their identity hit him for the first time.

Human beings!

It didn't hit him very hard. A strictly scientific anthropologist would have been more stimulated than he was. An emotional anthropologist would have just about fallen apart with excitement; that was an inner condition unknown to sophisticates like Steven. Steven had no specialist convictions. But he had been present, because he couldn't avoid it, when the subject of other races on other planets had been discussed by experts. And so the reality did impinge, and did hold him unmoving while he looked, and looked, for several seconds.

What he saw was that the natives of Mittend were not exactly white. There was some mix in them. That was the way he thought of it, because he was a little bit of a mix himself, and had on occasion referred to Steven Masters as being a citizen of the world—laughingly, of course. His great-grandmother had been a mixture of Indian and white; nobody knew exactly which quantities of which. Nor did they care, because she was a fabulous beauty. His grandfather had married a very pretty woman who had a touch of Chinese and Hawaiian in her. Steven's father had married a girl of German-Russian origin with black hair and a Spanish look to her. (Those Spaniards have been everywhere.)

What particularly fascinated Steven—and froze him —was not so much that the . . . Mittendians . . . were human, but that they *all* looked a little bit like Steven, seen close up. By the time he had savored that awareness, they were close, indeed.

His next realization was that he was running furiously, panting as he ran, sounding, and feeling, out of condition. He was climbing now; the hill seemed much steeper going up it from this side than it had seemed coming down.

Incredibly, at this late instant of time, it dawned on him that he had been foolish in venturing off by himself; such thoughts simply did not occur to him, normally. He did what he did when he wanted it, and to hell with it. But, now, for the first time a thought came: You madman, call for help!

He parted his lips a little wider; they were already open from each exhausted gasp. Through that enlarged opening, he emitted a small sound.

It was *so* small. It made an almost infinitesimal impact on the air. But what it did do was stir up a memory of a time when he had locked himself in the upper floor of the Masters five-story New York mansion; mostly used for storage, it had rooms for a couple of the younger male servants.

No one ever did quite succeed in understanding how he had got locked into the storage side. It took a key that you had to turn; and at fifteen, presumably, a boy should be smart enough to observe that it was unwise to lock a door from the inside, and then lose the key. (He had thrown it out the window, and pretended to himself that it had slipped from his fingers.)

Standing at that window later, as it was getting dark, he called out to an employee. At least, Steven claimed afterward that he had called out; and maybe he was genteel about it, and merely spoke loudly enough to be heard four feet away instead of ninety-four. But that was not his description of the event later.

Embellished, the account included the possibility that the man, whose name was Mark Broehm, had locked him in, and then had stood on the lawn below, and laughed at his discomfiture.

"He was just crazy down there, Dad. He must absolutely hate me, and maybe hates rich people."

His father, who had so many things on his mind all the time, this time wondered—for more than just split-instants—how come his son was the one who ran up against these strange, angry people. Briefly, then, he was motivated. As a result, for a minute, he talked at the boy.

He said, in effect, that truth was best. That the punishment for a harmful act or lie was automatic. You remained psychically connected to the harmed or lied-to person, and to that extent were not free.

Presumably God *and* Steven should have known the truth. But Steven, in fact, had the affair well twisted in his mind. It became the time when "one of the servants tried to kill me, for no reason. I only spoke to him twice all the time he was around. And maybe that's why. Maybe he felt rejected. Maybe he wanted some attention."

Out of the mouth of a fifteen-year-old came *that* truth. Maybe Steven wanted some attention from a perennially preoccupied father.

The memory, and the running, and the vague attempt to cry out—and the inability to—were a confusion of the end of a chase in which he was the pursued, and his pursuers were only steps away.

In those final few moments, as the strangers closed in on him, and reached, Steven cringed. It was an inner shrinking. The feeling was that unclean, alien flesh would for the first time since life began on Earth touch an Earthman's skin. He felt that thought in his every shuddering cell.

The next instant of eternity—it happened. A Mittendian spread of fingers brushed his right shoulder. Slipped off. Reached again, and this time caught him by the arm, and spun him around.

Deep inside Steven, something screamed.

"Mother, the touch, the feel—it's too much. There's a thousand names in this thing. Quick, move it!"

CRASH!

Steven stared at where the two glasses of beer lay on the dingy floor of the bar. From behind him, the bartender's voice came sharply: "Mark, what the hell was that about? Wake up!"

Steven turned. It was an automatic movement, part of an enormous confusion. In those initial moments, he did not think of himself as the person who had been addressed. But he thought vaguely: Mark? Mark who?

Almost blankly, as he turned his head, he saw the outside window of the bar. It had some words in black letters on it. Seen from where he stood inside, they were:

MOOR WOBLE

Moments later, still screaming somewhere in his interior, and still mental light-years from being willing for the rest of his life to answer to the name of Mark Broehm, he was lying on the floor.

CHAPTER 2

Never one to hold back his feelings, no matter who was inconvenienced, Steven began to yell. And he kept on yelling as people came over. The overall effect was confusion and dismay, as onlookers were startled and appalled by the suddenness of what had happened.

Somebody said, awed, "He's gone out of his mind."

Steven yelled louder. In the background, another somebody scrambled to a phone and called the police. But before the Law arrived, the screaming baritone (which even in Steven's demented ears sounded vaguely like the braying of a grown man sobbing and crying) evoked a second phone call, this time for an ambulance.

The ambulance attendants, when they arrived, found themselves in a desperate struggle with a Steven who kept shrieking the story of what had happened to him, and simultaneously resisting attempts to put him under sedation. In his desperate fear that he might be silenced, Steven fought ferociously, but he was finally held by two policemen while the ambulance attendant inserted the sedating needle. After that, consciousness lasted just long enough for him to be aware of being firmly carried, then gently eased onto a cot in the ambulance.

Naturally, he woke up (what seemed to be only) instants later. As his eyes flicked open, a quick glance established that he was in a hospital-type room. Even

16

as he swiftly found, and immediately pressed, the button that presently brought a nurse, he decided that his new approach must be less disturbing to his listeners . . . because they would continue opiating him if he were too noisy.

He told his story in a high-pitched voice to the nurse, then to another nurse, then to an intern, a doctor, and another doctor. . . . Finally, a psychiatrist came in. Also, somebody must have tipped off a reporter. And so, twice more, the hoarse voice of Mark Broehm tirelessly, each time in detail, elaborated on the improbable disaster that had befallen Steven Masters on far Mittend.

Later, a nurse brought the newspaper to him. There was his story alongside a news item which stated that subspace radio contact with the astronauts on Mittend had ceased early that morning, less than twelve hours after the mental disaster that had befallen Mark Broehm.

Reading that, Steven did not say to himself, What could have happened to my companions? That thought did not even cross his mind. His avid gaze was poring down the column, and suddenly he found what he sought. The precise words were: "An Associated Press phone query to the office of Steven Masters, Sr., brought the laconic comment from one of the billionaire's aides, 'We have nothing to say at this time.'"

"—*At this time!*" The phrase had a give in it, an implication of more to come, that in a single instant of time stimulated and relieved Steven. All the rest of the evening, and part of a restless night, he visualized "the old lady"—his term for his mother, who in her time had been a great beauty (and apparently could still get a charge out of her husband)—debouching her exhaustless emotion upon "the old bastard."

He thought gleefully: She won't let him sleep. . . . The mental picture he had was of a mother-type at once in a demented state of fear and anticipatory grief, insisting that no slightest clue to the safety of her darling son be left unexamined.

The fact that he was going on the expedition at all originally had just about unseated her reason. The truth was, his constant need to torment one or the other of his parents had been an irrational spur that caused him to persist in an adventure that didn't interest him at all.

She'll get him over here. . . . He went to sleep finally with that conviction. He awakened when a nurse and an attendant breathlessly rushed in to tell him that he was to be transported to a private room for an interview with two psychiatrists and—awed—Mr. Masters.

The transition from one room to another was achieved by Steven leaping out of bed, and with a protesting blonde nurse on one side of him and the helping arm of the attendant on the other, being guided down a gleaming corridor to a large bright room with one bed. There he yielded to adamant urgings and crawled into the bed. He was lying there a few minutes later when the door opened and—

Funny, thought Steven, he looks the same. . . . What was "funny" was that Mark Broehm's perception produced the exact Masters, Senior, that Steven remembered. It was a new thought for Steven. . . . For Pete's sake (amazed), these human bodies are all the same, and have the same equipment.

It briefly diminished him. During that shocked reaction, he told his story again but in a subdued fashion. For the first time in all these hysterical hours he actually thought about what he was saying.

He became interested, suddenly. The telling brought tiny curlicues of memory out of the mist of his unawareness at the time. Never one for introspection, he was almost unconscious of the strong wind of association that blew incessantly through his mind. Now, looking back—as he reported the details—the realization came.

Suddenly, he was amazed. In him—he observed—

stream of consciousness was a roaring river. For these brief moments, a basically intelligent mind looked, so to speak, with wide-eyed astonishment at the extent of the automatic madness inside him.

I'm really half-crazy. He had never had *that* thought before.

Almost as rapidly as the awareness had zoomed in, it now faded away. But the experience left him briefly subdued. For a minute or so he actually answered courteously the questions he was asked.

The boredom came back abruptly. He had been lying on his back on the bed, sort of relaxing. Now, he rolled over on his side, and glared accusingly at the elder Masters.

"Dad—what's the idea bringing a couple of lousy headshrinkers in to see me?" Each word pumped extra rage into him. He ended up yelling, "For Pete's sake, get these rats out of here!"

The billionaire climbed to his feet. "Are we through here, gentlemen?" he asked in a dignified tone.

The two doctors glanced at each other, and nodded. One said, "Substantially, we've got the story." The other one analyzed: "A clear case of paranoid delusion. Notice that quick hostility, sort of countertransference. However, I wouldn't rate him dangerous."

Steven snarled, "A clear case of stupidity." To the elder Masters, he said, "You going to let these two lightweights talk to the papers?"

His "father" answered in an even voice, "They will write a report. Whether or not I release it to the press is my decision."

Steven relaxed. "Be sure and show it to the old lady first—okay?"

Masters, Senior, did not reply directly. He walked to the door, opened it, and started through. And paused. Without turning his head, he said, "I suggest you leave the hospital as soon as you can, resume your previous activities as a beer waiter, and don't build up any hopes. Your story is fantastic. Good-bye."

He walked out, followed by the two doctors. Steven

lay back on the bed, a contemptuous, rebellious smile
twisting his face. And yet—he was shocked. Something in the old geezer's tone of voice. Could he have
meant it?

The rest of the day passed slowly. He was wheeled
back to his original room, where there were three
other beds besides his, and three nondescript (to
Steven) types occupying them. He continued to receive
casual treatment. Which meant no special instructions had been given about him. The shock grew.

Night came. And, presently, sleep time. And there
he was, still Mark Broehm, still caught.

Alone.

In the darkness, he lay sort of hunched up, on his
side but in a crouching position, as if to protect himself
from in front.

He lay there, feeling lost. Heavy, heavy was upon
him. . . . The body of Mark Broehm had gained considerable weight and had gotten older. It felt ugly, and
not-me.

But a thought had come: They were treating him
like a crazy person. He'd better watch it, or he'd be
forcibly restrained.

Cunning, scheming, sleeping, waking—that was the
rest of the night. How do you pretend to be sane, when
you're Steven Masters in the body of a man—a former
servant—fourteen years older? How, how, how? Oh,
what a bore.

Morning.

As Steven sullenly started on his breakfast of two
eggs, two slices of buttered toast, strawberry jam,
and coffee without cream or sugar, a rough, jolly-
faced, bright-eyed man came into the room, glanced
around, and headed toward Steven. Steven had never
seen him before; that was his first reaction. But after
a moment, an odd feeling of recognition came. This
was the owner of the Elbow Room.

His name—he had it—Jess Reichter.

The overweight, roughly dressed human being

waddled over to the bed, and grinned down at Steven. "Hey, Mark," he said, "you're in all the papers. We've got more business than we can handle, and I keep promising that you'll be back there slinging the stuff." Cajolingly. "How about it? And while the rush lasts, you get double pay."

Total insult. A sense of absolute outrage. The entire complex of get-even-for-this-if-it's-the-last-thing-I-ever-do. Mouth opening to blast. And then—

Just a minute. . . . The cunning thoughts of the night reached up from inside and flapped his lips together. —I may have to use this so-and-so (that was the sudden restraining thought) to get me out of here. . . . He'd need the Elbow Room to lay over in while he sized up his situation. Most important, it was the place where "the old man" expected to locate him.

"Yeah," said Steven. It was the best he could do.

Reichter said admiringly, "You always were an odd fellow, Mark. But you really made it great this time."

"Yeah." Steven smirked.

"That's the stuff," said Reichter, sounding relieved. "Stick to your story, hey."

"Yeah," snarled Steven.

The grinning fat man giggled, and began to back away. He waved from the door. "See ya, Mark. Soon, fella."

He departed hastily. And it was Steven, now, who was relieved. Because the impulse had come back strong, to leap up and smash out with his fist.

The interview depressed him. He thought grimly: Boy, if that old fool doesn't show up . . . if he swallows that paranoid stuff from those two shrinkers . . . The mere possibility that his father would do nothing was shaking. Because then he would be Mark Broehm. He who had been twenty-three suddenly would be thirty-eight.

A nurse came in after lunch and told him that he was to be discharged, and could leave any time.

That produced an immediate, rare (for him) feeling that things were not so bad as they might have been.

I could be up there on Mittend and a prisoner of those savages.

His good feeling dimmed considerably when he was taken to the cashier's wicket of the hospital and presented with a bill for $1,378.50. A thorough search of the pockets and billfold of Broehm produced two dollars in bills and eighty-three cents in coins, and—fortunately—two soiled, folded check blanks of the Fifth National Bank. Without hesitation, Steven used one of the checks to pay the hospital. The possibility that there might not be that much money in Broehm's account did not disturb him—not yet, anyway.

Outside, he walked down the steps. Then out to the sidewalk. There he stopped. He was beginning to feel the chill of the October afternoon. But he stood on the concrete walk, baffled. On his previous hospitalizations (as a child) there had been no steps that he, personally, had to descend. In fact, a wheelchair had taken him to a vehicle exit, and an ambulance had moved him in grand fashion to his home, with his mother following in her limousine.

Now—nothing. Reluctantly, already feeling frustrated again, Steven walked along the street into what soon became a dingy part of the city, and so to a phone booth. Shivering, he entered it and—for want of any other idea and struggling against rage—looked up the address of the Elbow Room.

It was 1643 Octonal Street. . . . Where the hell was that? He phoned the place, and explained his predicament to the admiring Reichter voice at the other end. "Hey," said Broehm's boss, "that's neat, not knowing where you are. You're really playing this great, Mark. I'll send one of the boys out for you."

"One of the boys" turned out to be exactly that: the younger (seventeen-year-old) of Reichter's two sons. The youth arrived in a jalopy station wagon; he was evidently accustomed to driving errands for his father.

He bowled along happily, and in due course delivered Steven into a part of the town that was as dilapidated as the Elbow Room itself, in front of which he came to a grinding halt.

CHAPTER 3

★★★★★★★★★★★★★★★★★★★★★★★★★★★

Steven played it blank.

It was a mental trick he had long ago developed to make time go by when he was bored. He had also used it to pretend that, though the body might be present, he wasn't.

He carried liquor glasses on trays, all the while moving like a sleepwalker. He spoke in a dead, even voice. He took orders and passed them on to the owner-barkeep in the same monotone. And said, "Yes, sir!" like it was a game.

Surprisingly, no one seemed to be disturbed. Or to regard his behavior as unusual. Grinning people kidded him: "Old man shown up yet in his Rolls Royce, Mark?" "Got your fair share of that billion yet, Mark?" "Mark— or is it Steven?—what . . ." And so on, ad nauseam.

Steven simply didn't let the meaning or the implication through the blankness. He knew why he was here doing this incredible work. Outside, it was cold, and inside it was warm. And he literally had no other place that he could go. He had of course always known that this was what held the jerks doing things, and he had always taken full advantage. Now, for a few hours, he was a jerk; and he was having jerk-level reactions. Boy!

But the balance of the afternoon swam past him through the blank. And so, also, the evening and the night. At 2 A.M. the last customer was eased out. Reichter fumbled around behind the bar for a while, took money out of the cash register, put on a jacket, and then a fall coat. Then he came over to Steven, and said, "In case you don't know, you sleep in the back."

"Yeah," said Steven.

"See you," said the plump man, as he walked off. At the outside door, he turned. "Your job is to clean up before we open at three. Remember?"

Steven watched him go out. The door closed. Then it jiggled, as if Reichter was making sure it was locked. Silence. An empty bar. Some of the lights had already been turned out, but it did not occur to Steven to turn out the rest. He headed slowly toward the rear, past the rest rooms, and came to a rear section that divided in two. To his left was a storeroom, piled high with cases of liquor. In there, also, were several spare refrigerators buzzing away.

To his right, a door. He opened it, fumbled for a light switch, found it, and when a bulb burst into brightness inside, he saw that there was a bed in one corner. Seeing it brought a tiny tendril of memory and recognition. . . . This *is* the back room.

Steven stood just inside the door, and counted up his tip money: twenty-eight dollars and seventy cents. The impression came through that that was a lot of money for a waiter in a cocktail bar like the Elbow Room.

So I've got bus fare to New York, he guessed. He didn't really know what bus fare was to anywhere. But that was his estimate. Enough money to get out of here and go to his New York apartment. That was the thought.

He lay down on the sleazy bed without undressing, and showed his teeth at the ceiling, and felt a seethe of returning rage against his father. He even made a *grrr* sound as he recalled Reichter's final words about cleaning up the place in the morning.

That'll be the day, thought Steven Masters, idly noticing that the ceiling of his back room was very high indeed, like the bar itself, and that there was another door leading outside, and some shelving that went all the way to that high ceiling, and—

At that precise instant, somebody knocked on the door. A woman's muffled voice said, "Mark, it's me— Lisa. Open up, Mark!"

Hey! thought Steven, as he leaped up, and bounded over, and unlocked and opened. He stepped aside, exhilarated, as a slender, youthful woman with brown hair done up in a bun slipped past him.

He closed and locked the door. As he turned to face her, she said brightly, "I bet you didn't expect to see me again, after that quarrel we had."

Seeing her and hearing her words evoked from Steven the same vague memory that he had previously had with Reichter and his son and the Elbow Room and some of the customers: a sense of familiarity but nothing more. What he half recalled and half reasoned now was that the quarrel had been basic. She wanted marriage. In response he had—what? It wasn't clear. But a dim conviction came that Mark had long ago married somebody, had deserted her, but had never bothered to get a divorce. So naturally it would be difficult for him to marry again.

Why she had come back after, probably, blasting Mark, she herself undoubtedly didn't know. But she had worked it all out like a woman in that little noodle. So here she was like an answer to a prayer that it had not even occurred to Steven to utter. The possibility that Mark Broehm would have somebody like this in his hinterland should have struck him, but it hadn't. The fact that somebody was doing something with all those other women out there had occasionally crossed Steven's mind; but not in any serious way. It was almost—though not quite—a new thought.

Everybody's got his little thing, it seemed. And this little thing had taken the trouble after the end of her own late-night job (she was a waitress) to drive several miles across the surface of the planet and to come into this back room to the embrace of Mark Broehm.

Seeing her, for a split moment it occurred to Steven that other people also desired happiness, pleasure, joy, excitement, and other good things; and—this was the philosophical part of his reaction—it was all right.

The feeling of acceptance was brief. Swiftly, the critical thoughts rushed back. Because, by his standards, she wasn't much. As Steven Masters, he didn't like her nose, part of her mouth, the lower half of her chin, her cheekbones, the slant of her forehead, the way she did her black hair—and, besides, he preferred blondes.

But he had already had the thought that he might persuade her to drive him to New York. Besides, what she had available—youth, a slim, little body, friendly eyes, and an affectionate way—she had right here, and she was willing to hand it over to Mark Broehm.

She turned out to be the type who required advance payment in the form of tenderness, pleasant untruths, murmurings of acceptance, and generally a relaxed atmosphere. Steven—with an inward sigh—decided he had nothing better to do. So, as was his wont with such, he really did an exaggerated preliminary, to the point where she was just about tearing the bed apart and rending the air with mating cries, when he finally turned out the light and began what he had always called "sex in earnest."

He was busy with that part of the transaction when a voice said in his mind, *"Now, it's dark. Reach over carefully, get the knife, and push it hard into his left side."*

Underneath Steven, the young woman freed her right arm, and reached . . . somewhere.

The voice repeated, *"Careful. Do it slowly, so he won't notice."*

Steven, in a convulsive movement of the Broehm body, rolled over on top of the extended arm, fumbled for the bedside light, and turned it on.

By the time this was done, Lisa was twisting. "What's the matter?" Her voice was bewildered. "What's wrong?"

Steven was holding her arm, and sitting up. From that position, using his other hand, he removed the knife that she had pulled out from under the clothes which she had casually deposited on the chair beside the bed. It was the only place she could have reached for such a purpose . . . was his evaluation.

Belatedly, the woman started to struggle. "Let me go. What are you doing? Where did you get that knife . . . ? Please don't kill me. Please."

Steven got up and put the weapon on one of the high shelves. Then hastily, with hands that trembled, he searched her clothes and her purse. All the time he was aware of her crying, begging voice. Aware, also, that she was probably innocent.

She was sent here to kill me, he thought. . . . It was the same type of voice in his mind, this time commanding, directing. A remote, analytical part of his brain had an identifying awareness: That was Mother, herself.

By the time he lay down beside the girl again, another thought had come. He should find out how *they* had got to her.

"Calm down," he said. "Somebody hypnotized you to come over here and kill me."

"No, no."

"It was you," he said, "who had the knife in your hand when I turned the light on. So let's start from there. Do you remember reaching for it in the dark?"

"No, no, no."

"Stop it!" Sharply. "Now, start thinking. What decided you to come over here tonight?"

"I-I suddenly realized I wasn't mad at you anymore."

His interview continued on that level. Lisa reluctantly identified the knife as the kind that was used in the kitchen in the restaurant where she worked. She did not remember picking it up.

Amnesia. "Mother" had utilized the human ability to be hypnotized. Steven, who had once dabbled with hypnosis and quickly found it tiresome nonsense, was temporarily not bored. In fact, genuine excitement came as he realized that Mother evidently didn't know that he was receptive to her lousy type of mental communication. He thought, exhilarated, I can tune in on that junky naïve stuff she dishes out. . . .

The triumph faded abruptly as another, more deadly possibility occurred to him. Maybe that tuning-in bit was true only with somebody Mark Broehm had known personally. But maybe it wouldn't be so with a stranger. A stranger need merely shoot him from a distance.

He could feel the Broehm face drain of color as that horrendous thought struck.

It was a badly shaken yet—after moments only—defiant Steven Masters who inwardly braced himself, and for the first time in his life realized that it could be, just could be, that he was going to have to start thinking about—what?

Beside him, the woman said, "Maybe I should get dressed."

"You stay right there," said Steven, with automatic grimness.

"I don't think after something like that, there could be any fun left," she said.

"Stop gibbering nonsense," snarled Steven. "You're interfering with my thought."

His thought was that he ought to have a plan in connection with . . . Mother.

In recent years no one in his right mind had ever suggested that Steven Masters ought to have a purpose in life. If such an idea had had the temerity to cross somebody's lips, Steven would have felt degraded.

When he had entered college—that in itself was a joke to Steven. But he expected to find pleasure there, and so he stayed, and did attend classes, and did graduate. That just about demolished the self-esteem of his professors, though they admitted he was obviously bright, and could pass in fact, if he ever applied himself or even handed in an assignment—which, naturally, Steven considered beneath him. Anyway, during the earlier days there, his father had been briefly lulled by the actuality of his son being in college at all, and as a result during some of his tiresome visits had suggested that Steven *consider* having as his purpose in college learning either business administration, economics, or both.

Obviously, after that, those were the two subjects that Steven avoided meticulously, almost—it might be said —purposefully.

And that was the last time anyone expressed any serious opinion that Steven ought to set himself a direction. After that, a chastened elder Masters had his attorneys discreetly sound out the university as to the size of donation that would soothe a shattered faculty's nerves. It turned out that each professor had a pet research project which, when funded by Masters money, seemed so worthy that, yes, for *that* he would suppress the bitter cries of his conscience and give a passing mark on the basis that, after all, Steven would never be called on for a practical demonstration of his college education.

What does it take to motivate a Steven? . . . It was happening—a little bit. To find himself with the outward identity of Mark Broehm . . . somehow, after that there was implicit in what he did and thought the *purpose* of becoming the real Steven Masters again. It wasn't desperately strong. He found himself extremely reluctant to plan—really—to go back to Mittend. In his mind it was vague, an impatience with the situation, and a half-expectation that it would right itself presently, automatically.

For about an hour after Mark Broehm's mistress had finally, in the wee hours, been allowed to flee into the night, Steven remained very angry. The rage had hit him suddenly as Lisa persisted in her idiot game of trying to get away. The need to punish was instantly so great that he became an insatiable lover. The girl-woman, sensing his mood, realizing that it required total—but total—submission, had responded with the extraordinary passion that only a combination of guilt and fear can evoke.

Now, he was alone. He lay in the darkness, seething, yet thinking. It was a deep, shaking thought: I'm in this madness to the death.

That stirred him. It touched a wellspring that transcended his identity as Steven Masters. He sensed a remorseless intention against him. . . . For God's sake, he thought, why *me?* Which was, of course, a typical Steven reaction. Somehow, all this should have happened to one of the nothing jerks out there in the distance. What happened to such people didn't matter even to them; Steven sincerely believed that jerks knew they were jerks, and were glad to have somebody club them to death and put them out of their misery.

Purpose came. He lay on his back, staring up at the ceiling of Mark Broehm's dingy room, dimly, dimly visible in the light that filtered through the dirty blind from a distant, murky corner light. He lay there, and he thought: I've got to do something about this.

He slept while that thought was still in his mind. When he awakened, it was there, waiting for him. It was purpose, formless in these early beginnings. The concept was so new that he kept feeling helpless, even hopeless.

But it would be with him henceforth, and it would grow.

CHAPTER 4

✦✦✦✦✦✦✦✦✦✦✦✦✦✦✦✦✦✦✦✦✦✦✦✦✦

"Hey, Mark—Steven—look!"

The voice came from behind Steven, as he was bending over a table and putting down a glass containing an Old-Fashioned with Canadian Club. It was the voice of Jess Reichter. So it was toward him, behind the gleaming bar with its bottles and glasses, that Steven—as he straightened—turned. The owner-barman of the Elbow Room was pointing toward, and through, the street window.

As Steven glanced along the line of that pointing arm, hand, and finger, he saw that a Rolls Royce had pulled up at the curb outside.

No question. No thought. Steven put down the tray, walked to the door and opened it. The coldness from outside hit him instantly. He winced, but he did not let it slow him. In seconds, he was outside and over to the car, as a chauffeur Steven knew as Brod (for Broderick Something, he recalled) climbed out.

"Hi, Brod, I'm Steven. The old man send you?"

There was a noticeable pause. The gaunt, uniformed driver undoubtedly knew the story of Mark Broehm. But, equally certain, he probably had not known what he was coming to.

"Uh, hi," he muttered finally. "You-a the Mark Broehm thing?"

"Yeah."

"You-a"—Brod faltered—"wanta drive to New York and, uh, see Mr. Masters?"

Steven walked over to the shining rear door of the glistening machine, and waited. Brod hesitated. When he finally came forward, he was white-faced. But he unquestionably knew what a genuine Masters heir would expect of him. He opened the door stiffly, and as stiffly closed it after Steven got in. Then he half stumbled around to the front seat, put the car in gear, and drove.

It did occur to Steven to look back and wave at the creatures of the Elbow Room. A mass of them were hanging out of the door of the hostelry. Steven had a mere glimpse of Jess Reichter struggling vainly to get past the numerous bodies that blocked him. His was a straining face in the background, strangely white-looking for such a normally red-faced individual.

The door opened by a combination lock, based on the date of his birth. Steven punched the buttons, and then as he heard the unlocking click, he pushed the door open and triumphantly walked inside.

Masters, Senior, followed him into the apartment. Steven was aware of the older man watching him, as he pointed at first one door, then another, and another, naming what was beyond it: the kitchen, three bedrooms, a music room, and library.

Abruptly, the ordinariness of what he was doing, the degradation of it, the frustration of having to be bothered with such stereotypes, bored him. "To hell with it," he snarled. "If you need any more proof, go and look for it yourself."

With that, he flung himself into one of the big, soft chairs, his back to the old "geezer"—that was the term he had in his mind. Behind him, the familiar throat-clearing process began.

"Oh, for Christ's sake, Dad," Steven complained. "With all your money, haven't you been able to get a doctor to get that phlegm out of your throat once and for all?"

There was a pause.

"The man you're talking to in that derogatory tone," said the deep Masters voice from behind him, "is noted for his logic, his understanding of human nature, and his refusal to be a made a sucker of by anybody but his son. In a small way you have made a case for the wildest story ever to come out of space. Therefore, the following events will now occur. You may remain in this apartment until further notice, and an allowance will be given you.

"I should tell you," continued the voice, that your story is considered incredible by my attorney and by my friends. However, as I have occasionally told Steven, I have a philosophy—"

Steven couldn't help it. "Every harmful act," he mocked, "will have to be paid for—" He broke off, bored, bored, bored, "For Pete's sake, Dad, stop it! "I'll sink into total apathy."

"My deduction is," said his father, "that what has happened to you, the *exact* nature of what has happened to you, proves that you did harm to Mark Broehm." He broke off. "That was a lie you told back there about Mark, wasn't it? He never did do what you accused him of."

"Hey!" said Steven.

He was startled. The two incidents had not previously been connected in his mind. What he remembered with a shock was not the long-ago destruction of Mark Broehm's reputation, but the fact that Mark *was* the last person he had thought about before the mind-transference occurred.

Swiftly, excitedly, in an absolute rage at Mark and at his parents for ever having had such an employee, he whirled around and described the sequence of events to the elder Masters, and finished, "Maybe that's how it works—the 'Mother' stuff. They switch your mind into whomever you're thinking about."

The familiar gray eyes watched him as he raged on; then, when he had finished, Masters continued as if Steven had not spoken.

"I have private information," he said, "that another expedition is going to be sent. And this is my decision. You will be on one of the rescue ships. It will be your task when you arrive on Mittend to locate the viable form of Steven Masters and release him from whatever unhappy condition you find him. His mother insists that I go personally, but that would be ridiculous. I point out to you that if your story is fact, then the task I am assigning you is probably unique. You will go and rescue . . . yourself."

Suddenly, the heavy face relaxed. "There, how does that sound?" "Father" Masters smiled.

It sounded persistent. Unattractive. Something about the tone . . . The old buzzard meant it. Steven did his blankness. And, while he was doing it, Masters, Senior, took a folded document out of a breast pocket, and tossed it accurately on Steven's lap.

"There's the report of the psychiatrists," he said. "I think you'll find it interesting." He added, "At my suggestion, they hypothesized that you were, in fact, Steven. And that's the result."

Steven lifted the paper distastefully, and threw it carelessly onto a nearby chair. "I'll read it later," he said indifferently, "if I have time."

His father hesitated. His manner indicated that he might make an issue of that item. Then he thought better of it. He walked deliberately to the door, turned, and said quietly, "Various groups connected with the new expedition will contact you. If it should come to my attention that you are not responding, or not doing what they want, you will be out of this apartment within twenty-four hours."

"Better not let the old lady hear you say that," said Steven.

The gray, cool eyes stared at him, unblinking. "After all," said the elder Masters, "your story *is* completely fantastic."

Whereupon he spun on his heel and walked out, closing the door behind him.

Steven sat.

He was startled after a while to realize that he actually had nothing to think about.

What did I used to do? The question produced a vagueness, an awareness of days spent in sleep, sex, drinking, tennis, eating, nightclubs.

No thought. No real interest in anything. Impulses quickly yielded to. Sudden outbursts of rage. Moments of instant hate. And a kind of constant waiting for somebody to offend him.

It occurred to him that, with Mother after him, he didn't really have time for stuff like that.

As these various realizations poured through him, he continued to eye the psychiatrists' report. And simultaneously kept resisting it.

The minutes went by almost blankly.

Finally, reluctantly, he reached. Picked up the paper. Leaned back with a distinct lack of eagerness. Unfolded the stupid thing.

The document began:

This evaluation is based on the premise that the principal purpose of the ego is the creation of a reality that will enable the individual to cope with his particular world. The world of rich-born Steven Masters offered a wider-than-average range of options. Of these, Steven elected what is best described in modern terms, elephantiasis of the ego—that is, total subjectiveness, modified only by his apparent awareness that it would be dangerous to commit murder, or inflict outright bodily harm upon other persons. So he was never an absolute monarch, arrogating to himself the power over life and death. However, within this lax limit, he abused his affluent condition without compassion, or mercy, and showed no noticeable affection for anyone, not even his parents.

In short, Steven managed to become one of the Big Stinkers of our time, apparently without even half trying. . . .

Steven reached that point in his reading and thought: Boy, I must really have got under their skins when I said what I did in the hospital. . . .

Almost at once, he had a second reaction: outrage.

You got it all wrong, guys. It wasn't easy. It was hard work. . . . The truth was, he had many times asked himself why he didn't just sink into the morass like the other stupes.

For Pete's sake, he thought, irked, it's not easy to be up all night. Not easy to pursue new girls when the ones you know are still willing to lie down. And it wasn't all that great to eat breakfast at midnight and dinner at nine o'clock in the morning. The unfairness of it rankled so much that once more he threw the paper down.

But he was glad to be back in the apartment. And, suddenly, more stimulated. Up he surged from the chair. He even played a few of his favorite records.

Maybe I ought to phone Mark's Joanie and invite her to come and stay with me—

Pause, while he remembered the knife. Sensation of some of the color draining from his cheeks. Then a shake of the head.

No, he decided. Mother got to her. She's poison.

The memory had a sobering effect. He shut off the phonograph. He had the grim insight that he'd better stay away from the people Mark Broehm had known.

It was getting dark outside, as he came to that decision. He could hear the servants in the rear of the apartment. Which reminded him that he had yelled and screamed and name-called all three, the woman as well as the two men. Because they were a singularly capable trio, it hadn't been easy to find fault.

What bothered Steven was the possibility that in some lousy cosmic department of justice shrieking insults equated with harmful acts. The fact that that particular department of justice had its quarters somewhere in the back of his own head did not occur to him.

But he was uneasy, suddenly. What bothered him

was that he would be alone in this apartment with three enemies this entire evening and night.

Hastily, thinking that, he retreated into his bedroom. After thoroughly searching the room, its clothes closets, and the bathroom (How can you "thoroughly" search a bathroom? Steven peered behind the shower curtain, and examined the walls for secret passages.), he locked both connecting doors, and braced chairs against them.

Later, when the woman called him on the intercom, and said timidly that dinner was ready, instead of telling her to mind her own damned business, Steven answered politely, "No dinner for me, thank you. I'm not hungry."

CHAPTER 5

****

Steven awakened the next morning in an untypical way, for him. It was, presumably, a Mark Broehm coming-to. A kind of peacefulness was in him, even a cheerfulness.

Steven, who as Steven usually slept with teeth making grinding sounds—so his girlfriends had reported—and who was mad either right away, or within a minute after opening his eyes, looked up at the great, high-ceilinged bedroom. It was all so normal that, for several seconds, he didn't even think of the madness.

During those seconds, his perception encompassed the luxurious drapes, the luxurious carpet, the magnificent bureau and desk, the wall murals, the ceiling murals, the chairs, and the settee. Then that same admiring perception slid back into the bed with its white sheets from Ireland, and its delicious woolen blankets from Switzerland.

Even when the horrid memory came—which it did, of course—he couldn't quite sink into abysmal gloom.

New York, he thought. He'd done it despite incredible odds, in five days.

I don't even look like Steven Masters. But here I am, accepted. And I haven't yet told a single lie.

Both awed and impressed, he nuzzled into the coziness of the bed. New York was beyond the windows on the other side of the gorgeous drapes. Each day from now on, it would get colder out there, yet remain warm and delightful in here. A fellow had to be damned sincere to have put over a stunt like that while presenting the outward appearance of a former employee.

Boy!

Thought of Mark Broehm's outward appearance brought a momentary depression. Mark, and what he looked like, was a subject he had carefully avoided. No direct glancing into mirrors. Instant turnaway if window glass started its occasional—when the light was wrong—stupid tendency to be a reflecting surface.

Yet, despite his evasive tactics, he'd already had a few sobering glimpses of the reality. So today, he thought, when I get up, and while I'm still feeling on top, I'll see what Mark is all about.

It was not that easy to get up. An hour later there he still sprawled. Yet in the end, about noon, he rolled over to the edge of the emperor-sized bed, and sat up. From that position he climbed to his feet and staggered over to the full-length mirror in the bathroom.

As it turned out, there were no surprises. What he had inadvertently glimpsed—and not wanted to believe—was, in fact, the truth. Mark's was an old (to Steven) mid-thirties' face. It was a fleshy face, not lean and tanned and beautiful as his had been.

Steven stood there in that bright light before the full-length mirror. He forced himself to look. When he had at last gazed to repletion, he said aloud, resignedly, "All right, Dad, all right. This I can't take. This is too much. I give in. I'll go to Mittend—"

Before he dressed, he called the kitchen, and said, "Breakfast in twenty minutes."

"Coming right up, sir," said a man's voice immediately.

"Thank you," said Steven.

After he had broken the connection, he thought about his uncustomary politeness both last night and this morning, and experienced a qualm of caution.

These people could be witnesses against me at a hearing, and prove I'm not the Steven they knew.

He shrugged finally. To hell with them! If I feel like it's no longer a good idea to punch somebody with a word or a fist, that's my own damn business.

In a peculiar, twisted way, he was outraged that they might actually expect him to do harmful acts, when, as a matter of fact, that wasn't the way it had been. In his mind had been a very simple, pure thought. The thought was that these people didn't count, and he did. By definition, it was impossible to do a harmful act to someone who didn't count.

Steven dressed, beginning to seethe as it penetrated that out there in the wilderness of space, somebody was judging *him* to be on the same level as the nobodies.

He ate breakfast as it was served by a yes-sir and no-sir and what-is-it-sir, uneasy-looking trio that had kept the apartment going while Steven was away on far Mittend. What a shock it must have been to them to find themselves suddenly back at work.

Steven had a couple of shocks himself. The three helpers, whom he had once considered to be the ultimate allowable in what age deterioration could do, were about as old as Mark Broehm. The shocking part was, he had said many times, "When I get to look like that, I'll just put a bullet in my brain." Steven was utterly revolted by anybody who looked older than thirty-seven or thirty-eight. So far as he was concerned such elderly types caused all the accidents on the highways. Age forty and up cluttered the good restaurants, and generally got in the way.

His fears of the night before seemed to have disappeared. It did not cross his mind that Nina, the cook, or Joseph and Bob, the two housemen, might truly be agents of Mother. Had he thought about it (which he hadn't) he might have noticed that the process of reasoning by which he dismissed them as threats was that past harmful actions ceased to exist when you decided not to do them again.

Steven finished breakfast. Beginning to feel bored, he went into the colossal living room, and on through to the connecting music room-library, where the giant window was. As he seated himself in front of the window he noticed the report that his father had given him the previous late afternoon. Curious, he picked it up, and reread the first page once more.

Good God, he thought disgustedly, those psychiatrists went to school twelve extra years, so they could write crock like that. . . .

The irritation got him back on his feet. He stuffed the document in a drawer of a gleaming sideboard table. Still stimulated, he picked up the phone, and called old cronies at random.

The start of each call became a progressive frustration to Steven. Because each callee hesitated as he heard the unfamiliar voice of Mark Broehm say, "This is Steven Masters in his new body. Come on over." However brief the pause, it was too long for Steven. Each time, he indulged in some instant blasting. That seemed to put some people off, because they either became difficult, or actually hung up on him.

Despite these several negations, by late afternoon couples and singles began to arrive. Each newcomer hesitated as he saw the Mark Broehm body. But Steven had been drinking, and so he didn't feel quite so involved with Mark's "ugly carcass"—as he gaily described it—and it didn't bother him.

Soon, the place was buzzing as of old. There was screaming music in the far west room, and voices, and laughing, and the clink of glasses all over the place. When, long, long after midnight, the last of the revelers finally oozed out the door, only a girl called Stephanie remained behind.

She was one of Steven's blonde sticks of sexual dynamite, and she hadn't argued when the Mark Broehm-Steven said to her in a low voice, "You stay later—okay?" At the time she didn't say yea and she didn't say nay. But there she was in Steven's bed when he came into the bedroom; and she was already casually undressing.

Steven was not too drunk to remember that he was a hunted man. What he remembered, precisely, was that sometime during the afternoon and evening and night it had occurred to him that people had brought guests. So occasionally he looked up into a strange face and into eyes that had an unfamiliar brain behind them. The thought was that before he retired he had better search the place.

With that thought, he headed for the nearest clothes closet. The exact moment he took his first step, something tugged at his arm. It was such an odd feeling that Steven turned.

The turn probably saved Mark Broehm's life. There was a hideous clatter of sound. A long line of splinters flew out of the bedroom door, to Steven's amazement.

He was not quick, then. It actually took moments for the meaning to penetrate. But he really needed that much time to turn further, and to see the flashes of brightness that came at him from behind the single settee that stood in one corner of the bedroom.

From her position on the bed, Stephanie threw a high-heeled shoe at the head that was poking up over the top of the settee. She missed—of course. But the man who was there must have caught a glimpse of something coming through the air. And he made the fateful response. He ducked.

What Steven did was grab a chair, and dart forward. So, when the head came into view cautiously, the chair did a smashing contact with the full force of Mark Broehm's rather heavy body giving it power and weight.

The individual Steven dragged into view turned out to be one of the strange faces. Since he began to stir almost immediately, Steven hastily—at the girl's suggestion ("I read it in a book")—tore the lower end of a bed sheet into strips, and did as good a tying-up job as he could manage.

And so, there, presently, lay the would-be murderer, eyes open and glaring at them. "I'm not talkin'," he said grimly, in answer to a request for name, address, and occupation.

He was a man about twenty-six, medium tall, sullen-faced, with stubborn, angry gray eyes. Steven systematically searched him. In his billfold was a driver's license with the name, Peter I. Apley, and an address on the lower east side. One of the cards he carried said he was a member of a photographers' association.

A vague memory was triggered. "Hey," said Steven, "you're that photog whose camera I once broke and—"

He stopped because he suddenly felt outraged by the unfairness. He was assuming that this was another of those harmful-act deals out of his past. . . . But, just a minute, what about *him* hounding me? It had been one of those lousy things where the photog haunted him day and night, climbed precariously up to windows, used a telephoto lens and other devices to get compromising close-ups.

Steven was dwelling on his put-upon feeling, when another memory poked through. Oh, that one, he thought, subdued. What he recalled was that after breaking the man's expensive camera, Steven in his get-even fashion had put his spies on the guy, found out his private life: Married. Girlfriend on the side. It'd been a distinct pleasure at the time to have the wife told about the mistress. Then, when everything was in an uproar, he made a skillful seduction of, first, the wife, and then the mistress, with those revelations skillfully accomplished, also.

Both women, with the usual (usual to Steven) madness of females, had taken it for granted that their minuscule charms had finally attracted what they had always dreamed of. (That's where the skill had come in, making the meeting with each one appear accidental, followed by an apparently anguished pursuit, as if an overwhelmed rich young man had, by chance, met his destiny.)

Neither woman seemed even dimly aware that a thousand other women had already crossed that bed. Naturally, he dumped them after achieving total conquest. If either woman could afterward pretend that she had a shred of feeling left for Peter Apley, she was a goddamn liar.

Steven forgot his own put-upon feeling. The memory had cheered him up. "How's Sue?" he asked. He was staring at the man's face as he spoke, but there was no visible reaction. Steven shrugged, and thought: That must have been some other jerk's jerky wife's name. . . .

He got up, and went to a safe in the library, where he kept his book of names and addresses. (Yes, he kept a complete record—just about his only personal labor.) He opened the by-now-respectable-sized volume, and skimmed through the A's. There, as he had correctly remembered, was Apley. The wife's name was Sarah, not Sue. The mistress was Anna Carli.

Steven nodded happily. Closed the thick looseleaf notebook, put it back, and locked the safe. Back in the bedroom, he said to the girl, "What do you think we should do with him?"

"Why don't you just drag him out into the hall?" she said brightly. "There was a book I read—"

It didn't occur to Steven that he might call the police. He took it for granted that Apley was another agent of the remote, deadly—but somewhat ineffectual—Mother, and that the guy was possessed, and not personally guilty.

The time was shortly after four A.M. when Steven, feeling pleased, deposited Peter I. Apley, bound and gagged, in one of the elevators. The door did its automatic closing. But of course the machine just sat there, and would continue to do so until somebody on one of the lower floors buttoned it into action.

Steven returned to his apartment.

CHAPTER 6

****

He came back, and the earlier concern returned with him.

It returned abruptly with a sobering realization that Apley had been a Steven-harmful-act, and not a victim of Mark Broehm.

As a consequence, there were precautions he'd better take.

He saw that, during his absence, the blonde Stephanie had crept under the covers. She lay there on her back, and gazed up at him with her hazel eyes, expectant. Steven stood over her, and noticed—as he recalled doing once before—that for him hazel eyes and blonde hair weren't right. He had always had the peculiar belief that genuine blondes were blue-eyed; therefore he determined that Stephanie was a product of beauty parlors and hair coloring. What bothered him now was that he really knew nothing about the girl.

In his own fashion, he was practical-minded. And, at an abysmal level of reality, a winner in his own right. He had long ago found out that many people were accustomed to rough handling. Some thereafter avoided the handler. But others merely tried anxiously to fit into what an angry person wanted, as if they believed there was rationality behind the anger. Since behind Steven's rages there was only Steven, in some respects they merited his consequent contempt.

Stephanie had always tried to adjust, and fit in, and be pliable, willing. But now that was not—Steven realized—a sufficient recommendation. In his mind, her past history mingled with that of other blondes he had known. He seemed to recall that she had been married twice; and that the second time she had left her husband it was because she believed Steven was interested in her.

But, fact was—he shrugged—that might not be her at all. That could just as easily be ninety-three other blondes.

Steven stepped up to the bed, took hold of the covers, and flipped them off Stephanie. For quite a few seconds, then, he simply stood there and gazed down at her slim nude body. He broke the silence curtly: "Sit up!"

Not quite like a little puppy, but almost like, Stephanie raised herself. Steven knelt on the bed; and ignoring the perfect female body only inches away, grabbed up the pillows. The girl's purse was under one of them. He picked it up, and emptied the contents onto the bed. He was looking for concealed knives, and other weapons. The purse had nothing but feminine things. So he dropped it, and fumbled over the sheets, then felt and shook the pillows.

Satisfied that there was nothing, he threw the covers back over her. Frowning, he stood above the bed. "I ever do you any harm?" he asked.

"You mean—did Steven?"

The question was spoken tentatively, and it instantly aroused in Steven the frustration of the previous morning when he had got all that silence on the phone. "Who else, you stupe?" he blasted.

Pause. Then timidly: "You're doing me harm right now, calling me a stupe."

"Oh, that!" said Steven, dismissing it. "What I mean is, did I ever hit you?"

"You knocked me across the room a couple of

times. It was not very nice of you." She spoke plaintively.

Steven stood there. For a man who had hit women whenever they got—as he had always put it—"bitchy," the impulse he now had was not easy even to think about. He wanted desperately to make amends without losing his dominant role.

He parried, "That all? Just a couple of shoves?"

"Well—" Her face did something hard to define. Memory was surfacing, and there was a great stirring all through her. Her body moved under the covers. She said in a complaining tone, "I have reason to believe you've been unfaithful to me."

"Good lord!" said Steven, involuntarily.

He was alarmed suddenly. He had a feeling he was witnessing the birth of a harmful-act syndrome. Until this moment this benighted creature hadn't dared consider that what he had done in the past was something he didn't have the right to do. But now, in his attitude there was a softening . . . she detected it. And she was moving in to take advantage.

"Listen!" Steven said urgently. "Will you accept an apology for those shoves?"

"Of course." Her voice was abruptly hopeful.

"I'll never shove you or hit you again. That's a promise."

"I'm so glad." Suddenly, there were tears in those large hazel eyes. She sobbed. "And you'll promise not to be unfaithful anymore."

A startled Steven stood there, and stared mentally at the speed of a female takeover when she believed she had a guy on the run. He had to consciously fight his resistance to what was happening. He said in his most positive tone, "Absolutely."

"I don't believe you." Her face was hostile. "You're lying to me," she said. "I don't believe you're Steven."

The situation was out of hand. And he had other things to do. He said, "Now, hear this, Stephanie. I'm going to search the apartment. If one person could hide here, maybe another one could, also. So, you wait right here—and I'll be back."

The girl said something else. But Steven had moved away, and didn't hear what. He went first to the settee, and glanced behind it. There lay the gun that had nearly riddled him. It was a thirty-eight, with a silencer on it.

Expertly, he released the catch on the clip, and drew it out. The clip still had two bullets in it. So there must be a third unfired round in the barrel. Enough for his purposes, without his having to open the secret drawer in the bedroom where he kept two loaded automatics.

Gun at the ready, Steven gingerly opened first one and then the other of the two clothes closets. From there he sallied forth to the outer rooms. Peeked behind chairs and settees. Poked into the cloak room. He even searched the kitchen and the storerooms in the rear. Reluctantly, he abstained from arousing the three servants, deciding that if an intruder was in there, that could be checked out in the morning.

I'll just lock Stephanie and myself into the bedroom, he assured himself.

As he finally headed back to his bedroom, his inner disturbance was, if anything, more intense. Apley's attack had exploded the hopeful hypothesis that only people against whom Mark Broehm had perpetrated harmful acts could be used by Mother against Steven, when he was Mark Broehm.

It wasn't so.

Apley was a victim of a whole series of vindictive acts, not by Mark at all, but by Steven.

What it added up to was that both men's past villainies were now combined.

Before he entered the bedroom, Steven had a thought about that—and removed the bullets from the automatic. He hid them under the cushion of one chair, and the gun under the cushion of another.

Then, feeling better, suddenly stirred by the potential of the female waiting for him in the bedroom, he pranced through the door.

He came to a teetering stop just beyond the thresh-
old. And stared wildly.

There was no sign of Stephanie. His gaze flashed
to where he had, earlier, noticed her clothes in a neat
pile on a chair. They were gone.

"I'll be damned," said Steven, loud and clear.

He didn't, of course, instantly accept the absence.
But in the end there was no question. In five
minutes or less of weaseling dialogue, he had transformed one of his pliable types—the only kind that
ever played the foolish game of hoping that by complete submission to the son of the world's richest man,
she would cause him to become so enamored that
something on the princess level would happen . . . he
had turned one of those from an easy profit into a loss.

It wasn't all that sad, of course. He was actually
exhausted. He started to sleep as he leaned toward the
pillow.

He awakened just short of noon the next day, with
the phone ringing. It was the first of the government
agencies. . . . "Just making initial contact, sir. Could
you come over this afternoon at your convenience, Mr.
Masters? Military-Space Research, Biologics Institute.
Electromagnetic Phenomena Department. Ask for Dr.
Martell."

Steven, remembering what his father had threatened
the day before, and remembering that two murder
attempts had now been made, reluctantly agreed that,
yes, he would show.

He despised scientists as much as he despised anybody—which was everybody—but maybe one of them
had just one bit of information he could use.

He needed something from somebody.

CHAPTER 7

★★★★★★★★★★★★★★★★★★★★★★★★★★

It was called biofeedback training.

"What we want—" said Martell. He stopped. He looked up at the ceiling. He shrugged one shoulder. His eyes acquired a glazed expression. He made a twisting movement with one hand. "—Want, is—" His mouth sagged open, and he stood there for ten seconds; then, seemingly unaware that he had paused, continued: "—Put this thing—" He laughed up-roariously as at some secret joke, or else the word "thing" had a humorous connotation for him. "—On your head."

Steven slumped into the indicated chair. He half sat, half lay there while a sort of helmet was fitted over his head. But he was thinking: If it's true that a scientist can know a discipline without having to be a good example of it, then I'm not wasting my time. . . .

His reassurance to himself was a paraphrasing of a statement made in a psychology class he had attended at college. The instructor who made the statement was teaching marriage counseling, although his students knew he was having marital troubles at home.

(Steven, perversely, enjoyed classes in which the credibility of the professor was suspect, or demolished. For such courses he would drag himself out of bed even on impossible mornings when he hadn't slept all night.)

Sitting there in the long, narrow room, he began to feel a lot better about this training program. The credibility was already close to zero. Though, of course, it probably was true that a physicist whose own television set flickered, and faded, might still know how to fix everything in a television station. Or a chemist could mix the elements of his science with masterful ability, but serve a lousy cup of coffee. Steven's personal doctor had an incessantly runny nose, but Steven always dutifully swallowed his prescriptions as if the guy could cure the common cold.

Somehow, Steven told himself happily, the hideous private lives and twisted personalities of scientists in general (and the ones he had already met here in the government training center, in particular) must not be construed as affecting in any way their skill as scientists.

"Have a thought that will turn that light green!" instructed the nondescript (to Steven) scientist in the clean white smock.

Steven found the thought, a kind of blank contemplation of a movie he had seen in his childhood, which just happened to come to mind. So long as he thought of that movie, the light remained green.

"Now, find the thought that will turn on this blue light!"

That turned out to be a time when he had become enamored of an older woman when he was sixteen. Surprisingly (surprising to Steven, who had been a male operator, beginning at thirteen and a half), she had resisted him. And he was furious.

As long as he kept his mind on his rage, the blue light, though flickering, stayed on. And so it went: green, blue, red, yellow—biofeedback, it was called.

He would (Steven gathered) eventually wear the helmet all the time. If he learned to sustain certain thoughts, a computer to which the helmet was connected by subspace radio would respond with—what?

They didn't say exactly with what. Wait and see. That was the attitude. Steven's impression was that these poor, stuttering nitwits thought they had something big. There was a suppressed excitement in Martell, an incoherent bubbling that repelled some deeper survival instinct in Steven, even as that other, superior self derived satisfaction from the obvious neurosis.

CHAPTER 8

★★★★★★★★★★★★★★★★★★★★★★★★★

At the moment of transition, the real Mark Broehm continued to try to make those movements which are involved in setting two glasses of foaming beer on a tiny table. In his mind was his anticipatory awareness that the two men who had ordered the drinks usually tipped fairly well.

Mentally, he was savoring the feel of the coins that, in moments now, he would slip into the pocket where he accumulated each day's take of tips.

At that moment it happened. He was being hurried along by naked people. There was a great, bluish sky and hill country . . . and a gasping tiredness from running so hard.

During those first minutes, the intruding sadness about the money actually transcended his awareness of the change. Like the waiter who goes off duty before he brings the bill to a particularly good prospect for a tip, and has to leave that pleasant task to his relief, it was the lost money that weighed on his mind when, as a prisoner with his hands tied behind his back, he loped across a rather attractive hilly wilderness.

How can a human being adjust to such a transition? It wasn't hard for Mark.

Any minute now (that was his thought) I'll figure out how and when I was given those knockout drops, and transported to—to—

It looked to Mark vaguely like a part of the middle western United States.

His whole life had been lived in that state of intense realism. Nothing surprised him. The world was what it was, and the people in it—he had his own negating opinion of them: sheep. In due course he would learn who his captors were, and what they had in mind for him.

That had to be so. Nobody did anything without a reason.

As he reached that point in his automatic assessment, his captors entered a forest area. They immediately slowed to a rapid walk.

Mark recovered his wind with surprising speed. So fast, in fact, that even he was puzzled. Of course, he did not yet suspect that he as a self was now aligned with a much younger body. (Steven had always balanced his nightly dissipations with almost daily tennis—not because he cared about exercise, but he actually enjoyed the game and played it well.)

There in the shadow under the long limbs of trees, Mark decided that what had happened must be a case of mistaken identity. The mechanics of it seemed rather obvious to a devious mind like his: The knockout drops were somehow given to him earlier. Then the blackout as he was serving the two good "tip" prospects. The rest, of course, was simple logic. Somehow, whoever came in the ambulance was planted, and had him whisked off into the control of—

Once more, with narrowed, baffled eyes, Mark glanced around him at the almost naked people who walked on either side of him, ahead of him, and behind him.

For Pete's sake, he thought, who are these guys? The sooner he established to their satisfaction that he was not who they wanted, that much quicker would he be back on the job.

It was a purpose. "Hey!" he said loudly.

No one turned. No one seemed to hear. The entire group moved forward intently along what seemed to

be a natural pathway among the rather densely growing trees.

All right, you so-and-so's, thought Mark grimly.
Whereupon he stopped short. At once he placed one
foot against a small ridge, and leaned back, bracing
himself against the expected tug from the men who
held the rope-ends that bound him.

As he did so, he spoke again, yelling this time. "Hey!"
he said. "Let's talk—uh-h-h-h!"

The groan was wrenched from his lips as he was
cruelly jerked forward. His captors did not slow, or lose
step. With irresistible strength, and with their strange
eye expressions (unpleasantly angry), they broke
through his pitiful attempt at holding back. Dragged
him at least a half dozen staggering, tumbling, sliding
yards. At which time (with a horrendous effort) he was
able to recover his balance.

During the long day, a shockingly convinced Mark
Broehm kept taking new looks at the people around
him. He came to a new, startling conclusion: drug
addicts. . . . Their eyes were the deciding factor. His
first impression—that the eyes showed hostility—
yielded to a developing awareness that the real truth
was they didn't look sane.

As the long afternoon came to an end, and twilight
settled over what had again become hilly brushland,
he and his captors emerged from the wilderness onto the
bank of a river. There, beside the gleaming, rippling
water was an encampment of other naked people like
themselves, except—wilder. Even less civilized looking,
somehow.

A few minutes later, he was greatly encouraged
when he was untied. But he was slightly degraded
when a man came over with a bowl of what turned
out to be thick soup, motioned him to sit (he sat), and
ladled the stuff into his mouth with what seemed to be a
wooden spoon.

When the meal was finished, the man pushed at
him. An uneasy Mark allowed himself to be tilted onto
his side.

He remained in that lying-down position most of the night, awakening several times to peculiar sounds. Splashing noises from the river. Animal grunts. A swishing and a surging and a grunting with great splashings as of large bodies breathing heavily and throwing themselves about.

It was pitch dark. Mark cringed. And waited. And listened anxiously. But gradually, as the huge sounds continued—and yet nothing happened—each time he grew calm. And slept again.

What progressively bothered him, with each awakening, was the absence of people from his immediate vicinity. He had gone to sleep, aware that men lay on the grass near him. The first time he came to, he strained to locate his guards. But there was no one he could see. No gleaming, almost naked bodies. No glinting eyes watching him.

A cunning thought came: Maybe I could get away. . . .

As he had that first, vague impulse, a large animal roared in the near darkness. To Mark's shocked ears it sounded like a lion. . . .

For Pete's sake, are we in Africa?

The fantastic possibility was reinforced by the snarling and howling and trumpeting that responded to the lion's roar. But, presently, that also subsided. And his troubled sleep resumed.

The next time he awakened, Mark took advantage of the darkness to yield to nature's demands. He discharged both urine and feces, sitting up for the latter act. He felt uneasy while he was so engaged, because he kept remembering that a group of women had been herded over to a height, which overlooked his bed and his toilet. Something about their bright, wild eyes had given him the impression that they could see in the dark.

It seemed to be a long night, but it finally ended. And in the morning there was everybody. The momentary delusion of the previous evening proved to have been exactly that, for the beings he saw were all

human; all in a small way resembled a particularly
obnoxious person for whose parents Mark had once
worked. But of course that had to be ridiculous. . . .
Mark could not clearly recall how a fifteen-year-old
Steven Masters had looked. But some older version of
him was what Mark kept thinking of.

Once more he got the bowl of soup ladled into his
upturned mouth. And his experience of the previous
afternoon kept him silent. . . . It was slightly startling
to realize that his captors were also continuing their
silence. During all those hours not a voice had spoken;
there had been only the bedlam created by the animals.

Of those noisy beasts, there was no living sign. However, somewhat downstream, and on the river bank,
there seemed to be remnants of large carcasses. Mark
could see white bones, rib cages, bony head structures
—of what was not clear.

Shortly after breakfast, the now much larger group
waded across the stream, and up the bank, past a steep
hill, and so presently out into the same kind of hilly
wilderness as on the day before.

By noon Mark had revised his opinion of where all
this was. Not Middle West at all. He had in his early
twenties hitchhiked to Arizona: the high (5000 feet)
chaparral country around Tucson, and the even higher
volcanic flats (7000 feet) along Highway 60 toward
New Mexico. His memory of the details was vague.
But he recalled that it had been wilderness.

Somewhere off the main highway there, he decided.
Back in the hills. Nudist camps.

That day went by. What was puzzling to him was
that, though no one carried a packsack, or even a pack-
age, on that second night there was the bowl of soup
again, and a plastic spoon for ladling it into his mouth.
True, he and his captors had come upon another
group of nudists already camped by a stream—
presumably, *they* could have had the utensils and the
soup base. But still—

He watched carefully the next morning to see if any
of the equipment was carried along. . . . It was

greatly relieving to his sense of logic when he saw that, in fact, everything was left behind. Simply left there on the ground.

Mark deduced triumphantly that these strange types had camping grounds which they revisited from time to time.

That third day was another all-the-way-to-dusk-time of marching through endless wilderness to still another camping ground with shadowy figures waiting beside still another glistening stream.

Okay, you S.O.B.'s, he thought, if you don't want to talk, Mark Broehm can match you, silence for silence.

The fourth day went by. But this time, as night drew near and as the large company of men and women moved toward the bright, distant flicker of camp-fires, there was a sound: gunfire.

Heavy cannon—it sounded like.

Mark trudged along uneasily as the fires, and the steady hammering of artillery, grew still closer. And louder.

For Pete's sake, he thought, appalled, why don't they put out those campfires? Are they crazy? Whoever they're shooting at will get their range, and blast them.

(At eighteen, Mark had served his unwilling term in the armed forces, and had seen firepower equipment in endless practice action. It had seemed endless at the time.)

Surprisingly, no one else seemed disturbed. His captors walked steadily forward through the scraggly brush and through the darkness. When they came to the camp, there as in the past they found a large group already encamped. And, as previously, they settled down in apparent peaceful co-mingling.

While the guns, or whatever they were, continued their hideous cacophony, a man fed him. The ugly red flashes, and the huge blasting noises, were off some-where to the near left, as Mark, grimacing but resigned in a tense way, opened his mouth each time the ladle was offered him. As usual, some of the thick, warm liquid dribbled down his chin and onto his stained clothes. But neither that nor the roar of the guns appeared to disturb the almost naked man, as he crouched peacefully beside Mark. He did not smile. He did not frown. He did not wince or turn his head. Fantastic.

It was that total nonreaction which brought awareness to Mark finally that (almost blank-minded astonishment) whoever or whatever these people were shooting at did not shoot back.

A swift feeling of relief. He was even able, presently, to sleep fitfully. And then—exactly when it happened was not clear—one of the times when he awakened, he realized that the artillery was silent.

After that, the night became like the others. Except that somehow he had a feeling that the approaching morning would this time be more significant.

The enemy, silent though he had been, would be out there. Somehow, Mark believed, that would have to be reckoned with.

On the fifth morning, Mark Broehm opened his eyes, and saw what he had already smelled: another stream. But also beyond the water was what looked like a tumble-down city. Instant inner illumination came.

That, he thought, is what they were firing at.

As usual, he was fed by a man. Was it the same man as the day before? As usual, Mark was not sure. He was so intent, he said, "Listen, do any of you guys know Steven Ma—"

S-slurp-p, a spoonful of soup was ladled into his mouth as he was speaking. He learned instantly, then, if he did not already know it, that it was unwise for someone who was in the process of eating, or about to eat, to speak at the same time.

He choked. He coughed. He sprayed soup into the face of his feeder, and over grass, and onto his own clothes.

When he finally came to, he was being firmly led toward the nearby stream. His body still felt twisted inside, his stomach and throat muscles ached.

God, he thought miserably, all that agony for just one second of forgetting where I was . . . and asking. a stupid question.

The little river flowed lazily between its green banks, and presently curled off out of sight into and among the shattered buildings of what had once been a city.

The close smell of the water made Mark feel good. He glanced questioningly at his guard, who had stepped back.

He's not holding me anymore at the end of a tight leash.

Mark did not waste any time. With a sigh, he sank down to his knees—and cringed, half expecting to have those merciless hands grab at him. (They'd never allowed this before.)

His arms were still bound behind him, so there would be no escape, no avoidance, if it happened.

Seconds went by, and no one touched him. Mark made no further effort to look around him. Kneeling at the grassy edge, he bent forward and down for his first head dip since his captivity. Anticipating the invigorating feel of the water, he opened his eyes wide and, with an expectant smile of pleasure, watched his image in the water move toward him.

The only thing was—the face that lifted forward from the bottom of the shallow water near the bank *was not his.*

Confusion!

In moments of stress, the human mind reacts in a very complex fashion, but the conscious awareness of the individual is not enhanced. Later, there is a considerable effect; this often includes a lifetime trauma of great power and with enormous automatic influence on behavior. But at the moment—

. . . Confusion, blankness . . . a distant disbelief, and just the barest flash of recognition.

The next instant he was in the water, and drowning.

Mark came to with the realization that several hands had pulled him out of a considerable depth. And that now he was lying, hands no longer tied, on something hard and rough.

Still alive, he thought with a weary sigh. Whereupon he opened his eyes.

It required many seconds, then, for him to grasp firmly that his body was lying on the raft that had been moored to the piling. To become aware that the raft had been loosed from the piling, and that it was now slowly drifting downstream and into the ruined city.

Mark twisted around to look back toward where he had been. What he saw was a number of his erstwhile captors standing on the river bank, staring after him.

"Hey!" he called weakly. "What's the big idea?"

Nobody answered. Mark parted his lips to call again, then he closed them, and simply stared. Seen even from this outside vantage point, the scene that he was looking back at was absolutely fantastic.

An entire encampment of nudists. Naked bodies moving, turning, walking, gliding, bending against a hilly background in the near distance, and, far away, a gray haze of mountains.

The raft was caught abruptly by a swift current, and it spun behind an outjut of a broken building. It slowed almost immediately, and drifted to one side.

But in that one swirl of faster movement, he had lost sight of the camp.

The raft moved on carrying its solitary cargo into a destroyed city.

CHAPTER 9

The small group of men climbed separately out of the spaceship, Steven first.

He hadn't been too happy when Captain Odard had said, "After all, Mr. Masters, you're the only one who's been here before. We defer to your previous experience." But, still, it wasn't that big a deal.

All right, all right, I'll go first.

So there they all were on the ground: seven individuals in this initial landing craft. There were four other landing modules, waiting in orbit with the freight-train-like spaceship—which consisted of more than a dozen large, separate transport drums, each with its load of supplies and each with its crew. In due course, fifty-four more men would land on signal with their weapons.

The captain, a chunky man of much the same build as Mark Broehm—but physically tougher—came over and stood beside Steven.

"Hope you don't mind, Mr. Masters," he said, "if we keep a special eye on you."

"Don't worry," said Steven. "I'm tamed. The first time around convinced me. No more private jaunts over the hills and dales."

He walked gingerly to a canister that lay abandoned on the sand. Then he glanced up to the line of hills. Everything looked jarringly the same.

Right over there, he thought. That trio of hills. . . . He stared, sobered by an intense sense of reality.

There, several hundred feet to his left, was the original spaceship. Silent. Deserted. No sign of its crew.

And here—to his right—the newly arrived module, with *its* crew still very much in evidence.

He gulped in a breath of cool Mittendian air, noted absently that it seemed cooler than the last time, and therefore winter must be coming.

Better mention that to the others. . . . Like a good little cooperative type, he turned to say the words to Odard, but saw that the captain had wandered off. Steven could have activated his intercom. But little flashing lights on it indicated that several people were already talking to each other. . . . So, okay, later for that!

As far as he could see, there was not a threat in sight. Equally relieving that, for today at least, nothing aggressive would be done against whatever was out there beyond the horizon.

There was, he knew, a plan. Oh, yes, indeed, the plan was there, carefully worked out by military minds. An air scooter from their landing craft would be disembarked and given a crew. It would skim over every horizon, and then when its crew had located a group of Mittendians, an attempt would be made to capture one of them. Thereupon, the other humans would land.

The air scooter crew would include Steven on alternate days, a pilot, and two men with capture equipment. The attack force would, of course, be armed, and its members would—again, of course—act with the aggressiveness and disregard for their own skins that armed forces everywhere had always required of human beings.

When the other craft landed, there would be more forays. With always one group guarding the camp, prepared to fight to the death.

Whenever he considered those stringent orders, Steven experiencd a confusion. He could see that such a program was necessary—for soldiers. But in his mind, somehow, soldiers were . . . others. They were not he; and, in a peculiar fashion, for the time being at least, he felt reluctant to have even Mark Broehm treated as a disposable unit of such a force.

Made gloomy by the prospect, he watched half interestedly as the two men who were to accompany him —Ledloe and Erwin—came over and did some tests on the canister beside which he stood. For a long moment what their activity implied did not penetrate. Abruptly, it did. At once, as if he had become curious about something nearby, he turned and walked there. Then he walked farther. Then he hurried around to the other side of the ship, and waited there, shuddering, for the explosion that, fortunately, did not come.

But the thought was: All those minutes standing unthinking beside a leftover from the previous expedition that could as easily as not have been bugged with death.

God Almighty, Steven Masters, are you ever going to start thinking about such things ahead of time?

The details of landing and testing took most of the rest of that day. The air scooter was gingerly eased down from under its flap. The power was operated experimentally. Controls were checked out. The next day's flight was simulated.

Everything worked.

Night. Half the men slept aboard the module. The other half—plus one—bedded down in sleeping bags on the ground. Who did which had been decided by the drawing of different lengths of grass blades. Steven drew a sleeping bag and a night outdoors. What was disturbing about that (as much as doing it) was that he had always rather fancied his luck in such matters. But he worked it out.

Boy! he thought. This body of this guy, Mark Broehm, hasn't got anything going for it at all.

He lay awake for a while. Among other distractions of the dark was a point of light in the southern sky that somebody said was Earth's sun, and he stared at it.

The hours of darkness passed uneventfully, and swiftly. Because he slept through most of them.

Breakfast. Then the air scooter lifted away on its softly hissing jets. This time Mark Broehm's body was lucky. Because he was one of the four men who stood on the ground and watched it climb slantwise into the sky, and then watched it grow smaller in the distance of a blue sky that had little fleecy clouds in it.

Those who remained behind had small jobs to do. These tasks consisted principally of getting more gear from the module over to the camp. Morning went by.

Noon. Lunch. And then—

A speaker clattered into voice. It was the voice of the pilot of the air scooter, calling shrilly: "We're coming back. Stand by. We've captured a young woman. She's fighting like a demon. Completely insane. Stand by for a rapid landing, and come aboard to help!"

One woman, thought Steven, lightly dismissing it.

He was still thinking about it tolerantly when there was a yell. A man pointed at a dark spot in the sky. It was the scooter, and it came down a few minutes later. It hit the ground with a palpable thud, and its doors fell open.

Steven watched curiously as his three companions charged aboard. He still did not budge, though he heard the sounds of violent struggle inside. But a tiny thought did come: Has she been fighting all this time? . . . That shocked. The endurance of it, the fact that her muscles did not become exhausted. Inhuman.

What happened next was not easy.

It took four men to hold her, as she was eased through the door. One held her head—she tried repeatedly to bite him. Two were on either side, each clutching an arm and a shoulder. A fourth put his weight on her feet.

Even with that she wriggled, and twisted, and threw herself madly, and tried to avoid the needle that the fifth man—the medical aide—presently sank into her thigh.

Then they waited.

A minute—and she was still fighting. Two minutes. Three. She began to weaken. At the end of five minutes, she was still.

As she lay in what they hoped was a state of both drugged body and hypnotized mind, Kirliann images were projected at the electromagnetic field around her body, and simultaneously the English language was fed into her ears by a training device.

In the fantastically short space of an hour she was awake. There she lay, bound hand and foot. Whenever someone came near—which they kept doing—she glared, and showed her teeth. And snapped those teeth at the individual like an untamed animal.

As night came, her eyes glittered with a wildness that shocked everybody. "Christ," said Ledloe, "we'd better keep an eye on that dame. If she got loose during the night, she'd murder us all."

It seemed instantly true. Even Steven slightly modified certain thoughts that flitted through his motivational centers.

It was agreed that they would keep watch. Each man was assigned two shifts of thirty minutes sentry duty. They worked it out so that a timer would awaken them, in turn, through a hearing device in the ear.

That was designed to buzz in case a predecessor accidentally fell asleep during his thirty-minute vigil. Mark-Steven, who wasn't afraid of wild girls, noted down his two sentry times with a twisted smile. In the back of his head was a plan for when his first turn came to watch her.

. . . His timer buzzed in his ear, awakening him in darkness. He waited, expecting the man he was to relieve (Johnny) to come over and push at him. When no push came, an alarm pulsed through him. Slightly faster heartbeat, quicker breath, nervous movements.

Steven rolled over cautiously, and got his gun. From a knee position, he surveyed the camp. It was dark all right, but the stars were up there. After a minute or so, he could see the body shapes.

He counted them, and they were all there, including

the girl, including Johnny—lying down. Asleep? It had to be so. The sentries were supposed to sit up during their half hour.

He crawled over to the girl. Her bright, open eyes stared at him as he lifted her tiny skirt, exposing her. As he readied himself for the act of rape, there was no analytical thought in him about consequences. He didn't say to himself, "I am about to commit a harmful act against a Mittendian, and thus enable Mother to use her against me—"

Steven operated on a simpler level of logic than that. What he was saying-feeling to himself was, "Here I am more than a dozen light-years from Earth, never for a second expecting that I'd be able to get a girl again until I returned home. But I'm going to get one. I'm the only person here who understands things like that."

He was that stupid. That unthinking was Steven, as—actually—always.

As he maneuvered himself in the dark, first straddling the girl with his knees, it did not cross his mind that the last time *he* had been touched by these Mittendians they had reacted with horror and shock at whatever transmitted from him to them.

To Steven, the reality was that this female was being neatly held for him (in a manner of speaking) by his pure—simple-minded—companions, in that they, without ulterior motives, each man with a past history of honor, integrity, loyalty, bravery, and a sense of duty, had helped capture her and helped tie her up.

Their purposes with the girl were well-intentioned. They wanted to calm her wildness, to reassure her, and thus in time persuade her to communicate with them as one civilized being communicates with another.

Steven understood all that, and in his fashion was quite willing for it to happen, also. Indeed, he even had a fantasy in which he pictured to himself that his method of communication was the one that would actually solve the problem. . . . She'll fall in love with me—

Girls on Earth had a habit of doing that after he

had mistreated them. Thus, they disgraced themselves with their former friends, and, of course, he quickly discarded them, and never gave them another thought, or even clearly remembered them if he ever saw them again.

Thinking all those madnesses, he lowered himself upon her, and felt the touch of her skin, and started to press down. The writhing, twisting, resisting body felt pleasant to a long-time semi-rapist like Steven. Steven belonged to the school of males (of Earth) who believed that all females were sluts at heart, and wanted a man to force them.

He was careful to stay clear of that biting, snapping mouth, but pleased that she made no other sound, spoke no word, yelled not. She did breathe hard, and—justification—responded by producing a sufficient vaginal oil so that the process of lovemaking was thereby facilitated.

The act completed, Steven carefully lifted himself away from her, replaced her clothing, and was crawling off to one side, when—

"Mother—switch me!"

He was lying on his back, tied hand and foot. In the near-darkness, he was able to see that Mark Broehm was climbing to his feet. As Steven watched, confused, still not quite adjusted, Mark took out his gun, ran to each of the other three bodies on the ground, and there was the tiny plopping sound as he fired the automatic, aiming each time at the head.

One man groaned; that was the only other sound.

Instants later, the wild girl was back beside Steven. Obviously, then, whoever was manipulating her was expecting a lot.

Mark untied the legs of the woman's body, and then bound Mark Broehm's legs at the ankles. Then Mark rolled the girl's body over on its side, and untied the wrists—shoved the gun into the girl's hand.

"Mother—switch me back!"

The mind-switch that occurred the next moment affected them both.

But Steven was quicker.

As his consciousness wavered, and then came out of its blur, and he realized he was Mark Broehm again—he'd had no obvious thought or association during those fateful seconds that might have taken him elsewhere—he leaped.

With both feet tightly bound, he nevertheless jumped with all his strength.

He got her. He grabbed hold of the gun. And they fought there in the darkness. They were two silent beings, breathing hoarsely, but not yelling or making a sound. What was at first unbelievable was that she was as strong as a man. It was incredibly hard to hold her slippery, naked body while the two of them tugged in deadly earnest for possession of the automatic.

Silence, night, fear . . . Steven dared not cry out for the help that was available from the three men sleeping inside the module—dared not, because he had no satisfactory explanation for the three murdered men outside. . . . It was all too fast, no time to concoct a story, so much happening, the desperate struggle—

He held on; that had to be first. And, suddenly, a strategy that worked. Held on, and pushed with all the force of both feet—and lunged with his heavier Mark Broehm body against her.

It unbalanced her. He could feel her abrupt uncertainty. Instantly, he jerked at the gun with every ounce of his strength. Got it. And struck savagely. (Steven could strike women. He had struck them many times when they irritated, with, of course, only the flat of his hand, or a fist.)

His grip had been on the barrel of the automatic, holding it away from him. So, now, that's what he clutched. And it was with the butt that he struck her over the head.

She went down limply.

A jittery Steven, seemingly all butter fingers, fumbled at the cords that bound his feet together. As the knots yielded one by one, he was already making up a story that would pass—if he could depend on the power of the Masters money to prevent lie-detector devices from ever being focused on him.

The money had been enough, when the attorneys of the guy with the steam car had tried to force a lie-detector test on him—

Pause. Confusion.

Steven blinked, for it was broad daylight.

It would take a little while (there was genuine shock to dispose of) but in relatively short time—in about eighteen seconds—he deduced that he was back on Earth.

It required a slightly longer time (nearly two minutes more) to remember his last thoughts on Mittend, and to look around somebody's home music room, and to step up to a mirror and take a swift survey of a man's face and body, and to glance into a desk drawer, where there were letters addressed, some of them, to Daniel Utgers and others to Lindy Utgers. . . .

And to think, finally: Well - I'll - be - a - son - of - a - gun - good - old - dad's - lousy - philosophy - came - through - again - right - on - the - nose.

CHAPTER 10

✱✱✱✱✱✱✱✱✱✱✱✱✱✱✱✱✱✱✱✱✱✱✱✱✱✱✱

There are people who say you should consider life a game to be played cheerfully. Others advocate what they call positive thinking, with the admonition not to let anything get you down. Still others are proponents of winning: a winner—this group tended to point out—automatically feels better than a loser.

It is possible that all of these systems could have claimed Steven as an example of their ideas. Steven did each and every one of these things at all times (and he didn't even know that what he did was a system).

In a manner of speaking, he had always landed on his feet, and felt fairly ebullient about it.

No modest winner, Steven. Having won, he grabbed for the spoils of victory—and took it for granted that any penalties heading his way as a consequence of the methods he had used to win could be dealt with later.

As now.

Twenty-eight, eh? Steven felt surprisingly cheerful about that. . . . Getting younger, he told himself optimistically. The erstwhile steam car driver, whom he had pursued so vindictively, was—he found himself realizing—an exercise fiend. The resultant body was in a splendid energetic condition, and positively shining with good health: slim, muscular, vibrant.

Since Utgers also had above-average income, the combination of physical effectiveness and financial-business capability had attracted a good looking, bright-eyed girl who, still, at twenty-six, wore her blonde tresses long. The overall of her made her attractive even to Steven, and so, briefly, he was not in a hurry. It took two nights of getting acquainted with his—wife —before he came to his usual ennui.

Actually, there was another reason for his swift feeling that he had had enough of this place and this woman.

Late on the second day a newspaper headline announced a news release about Mittend, as issued by the Space Authority. The death of the three men was reported, and the escape of the captured girl, who had apparently run off into the darkness after using the pistol of Mark Broehm to shoot the three human victims.

It was accurately reported that the disaster had taken place while Mark was on sentinel duty. But the survivors had not, to date, been able to obtain a sensible story from him.

The news release, itself, made no mention of the earlier publicity by which Mark Broehm claimed to be Steven Masters. However, the media was not so reticent. They replayed the drama for their readers and —in the case of TV—for their viewers, leaving no scrap of possible information or speculation unprinted or unuttered.

What bothered Steven about the news release was that he had a feeling that the Space Authority knew more than it was saying. His conviction was that they had been advised by Captain Odard from Mittend that Mark Broehm was insisting that Mark Broehm was Daniel Utgers.

Accordingly there would be repercussions, it seemed to Steven.

On the third morning, he got up, and announced that he had business to attend to out of town. He ate breakfast. Then he went outside and got into the car, and drove off. To New York.

He drove to Steven Masters' apartment (where he had stayed as Mark Broehm), manipulated the lock-system, and took possession. From there, he phoned his father on a private number. When the familiar voice came on, he said, "Well, Dad, I'm back—this time as someone else. I'm at the Stig—"

The reference was, of course, to Stigmire Towers Apartment complex.

"I'll be right over," said Mr. Masters, Senior.

There was a hastiness in the way he spoke that telegraphed to Steven that the old buzzard already had all the available facts from Mittend. And truth was, it had been just such a possibility that had motivated him to his (relatively) quick contacting of his father.

As Steven replaced the receiver, he heard a door behind him open. An odd, suspicious thought passed through his mind. He swung around with a single, swiveling motion, and identified . . . Joe.

The servant stood in the doorway. He had an automatic pistol in one hand. An expression on his face telegraphed a peculiar kind of understanding.

In a convulsive gesture of his body, Steven flung himself to one side. The first two bullets probably came close to where he had been instants before.

The second two bullets tried to follow him as he rolled over and over on the floor, and flung himself behind a settee. From its doubtful shelter, Steven screamed, "Joe! Mr. Masters, Senior, will be here in twenty minutes."

If the meaning penetrated, it didn't reflect in the words which Joe now uttered. "Come out from behind there with your hands up!" the man's voice commanded.

Steven had already crawled swiftly and silently on the carpeted floor to the far end of the settee. He wasn't about to place himself at the mercy of a madman who had already shot at him four times. Somehow, Joe had had an intuition as to who this intruder really was, and years of hatred were pulling that trigger.

Even as he had thought, there were two more plops. This time, the bullets, instead of ripping noisily through wood, made the softer thudding sound of going through the padded part of the other end of the settee, where Steven had been a few seconds earlier.

Joe yelled, "Come out now! Come on out!"

Steven made no reply. He was gathering himself. The entrance to the corridor that led to his bedroom was ten feet away. He drew a single deep breath. Then, from a crouching start, like a runner starting a hundred-yard dash, he flung himself forward.

The mathematics of such a dead run were ninety-nine and nine-tenths percent in Steven's favor. Even a merely good runner can do a hundred yards in eleven seconds, and that was probably Utgers' speed. It was possible, then, that Steven actually did his first four yards in less than a second. Human reflexes are just not that fast. Many, many instants after Steven was already safe in the corridor, and in fact when he was on the point of entering his bedroom, he heard two more plops.

Theoretically, the stupe had now used up his first clip, and might not even have another, but Steven took the time to close and lock the door. Then he was over at the secret drawer. Moments later, clutching a .32 caliber Browning, he unlocked his door, took a swift glance around the corner of it, and, when he saw no one and heard no sound, he stepped forth.

He was in a fury, and temporarily without fear. He emerged from the corridor end without pausing, ready to shoot. There was no one in sight. But an open doorway indicated where the so-and-so had gone—off to get another clip, he deduced.

Steven arrived in the kitchen at a run, and there found Nina struggling with her husband. They were arguing bitterly, and she was trying to get the gun from him; they were briefly unaware that someone else had come in.

The woman saw him first. She immediately went limp. Her husband must have realized that something was wrong, because he stiffened, and then he slowly turned. At Steven's gesture, he sullenly tossed the automatic onto the floor. Steven walked over and picked it up and said, "Mr. Masters, Senior, will be here in a few minutes. I want you packed and ready to leave by the time he gets here. He'll pay you off. Tell Bob—same for him. Now, get!"

They edged away, the woman crying. "I don't know what got into him," she sobbed. "I told him just to ask you who you were, and—"

Steven presumed that Joe had indeed been rendered "out of his mind" by 'Mother'. But— "Out!" was all he said. "All of you!"

He stood by a little later as his father, after listening to the story and looking at the bullet marks, nodded his agreement. The older man paid off the by-now-silent trio. Both men stood by and watched them trudge out of the rear entrance of the apartment. Steven locked and bolted the door behind them. It was as he walked back to the living room close on the other's heels that he realized a grim truth.

This whole affair had a different feeling. With three men murdered, the feeling was that things were not going to be as easy as before. He had what—for Steven—could well pass as a sensible thought.

In its small way it was, accordingly, a milestone moment. But it was one more sad commentary on human nature. It once more suggested that the birch rod applied for good reason, and the instant penalty for a crime, and an equal law for everyone (but somehow without lawyers) was still the ideal way to deal with individuals of that strange, intelligent race spawned on the third planet of a yellow G-type sun, located near one edge of the wheel-shaped Milky Way galaxy some 36,000 light-years from the center of that wheel. Namely, the inhabitants of Earth.

When a man has been twisted all his life, his first rational thought—even a single tiny, tiny one—has got to be significant. That one straw of reason can, in a bright enough light, cast a long shadow line into the future . . . with implications of better things to come. More sense. More responsibility. The relatives, and friends, and parents (if any), if they have been holding their collective breath, can gulp in a couple of mouthfuls of hope.

Steven's rational thought: Utterly impossible to justify his real role in the murders on Mittend. . . .

That was quite a self-admission for a person who had not, since childhood, consciously agreed that he had been wrong. For Steven the problem he faced had a stark simplicity to it: Okay, I did it. Now, how can I cover up?

What was different from the past was that he had never before actually accepted the facts of a situation. The instant twist blamed the other person.

A few past patterns remained, of course. As usual, Steven had not given much thought to the matter until the news announcement the evening before. It was a pretty useful ability. Accusers who had confronted Steven in past times and crimes were astounded to discover that he had put the whole thing out of the forefront of his mind. After that, only the twist came out, except that under stress conditions it all flowed through his mind in an endless free association. At such times, he was usually too busy to think about it, or notice it. Invariably, he was quite nonchalant, for the simple reason that his attention had gone elsewhere.

The two men—father and, presumably, son—were in Steven's apartment. Despite the older man's effort, they did not during their entire dialogue face each other. Which was, in itself, partial evidence that the strange youngish man was indeed Steven. The elder Masters could not recall a time when Steven had faced another person. He presumed, wryly, that the exception must be girls in the clinch position.

But it was, in fact, a reasonably direct confrontation. Steven lay sprawled on a couch in his nonchalant fashion, and Masters, Senior, paced up and down— which was *his* way. He stopped occasionally, and gazed down distastefully at the person lying on the couch. But he listened.

Steven's story reflected his cover-up plan but did not deny the facts altogether. "It was so dark," he reported. "I sat close to that stupid female. Suddenly, she moved her whole body, and one of her feet slammed against my hand. Apparently, touch is what does it. Next thing, here I was."

As for the murder, Steven surmised that the bewildered Utgers had been used in some way to free the girl.

He shrugged. "That's all I know."

His exasperated father snarled, "In view of what happened the first time, with Mark Broehm the other person, why didn't you have more sense than to get that close?"

Steven said, "Why didn't they have the sense not to use me for sentry duty at all? You don't think I wanted to be out there at 2 A.M. in that pitch night."

That part of the reply must have had a certain degree of truth for the elder Masters. He stopped his pacing, and stood for a time staring out of the window at the great city below. Abruptly, he walked to the phone. The conversation that ensued did not entirely escape Steven Junior. But all he ultimately got out of it was that the other party agreed to contact the Space Authority immediately and arrange a meeting.

The meeting was set for that afternoon, which should have indicated that somebody, at least, thought there was a certain urgency about the whole thing. Steven was willing. But as he climbed out of his father's car and saw that they had come to one of those peculiarly ugly buildings that military people erect wherever they go, he had an instant intuition about the place and refused to go in.

The elder Masters made it simple. "You don't go in there, you're out of your apartment."

Steven climbed back into the limousine, and took the private phone off the hook. "I'll talk to them from here. You can tell them I'm not going into prison-type buildings with armed guards in them."

"Surely, there's no one in there," argued his father, "that you've ever harmed."

"This whole thing has got too hot for me to take any chances. For all I know, every one of the officers we're supposed to talk to takes it as a personal insult that you got me out of doing my stint in the army, and maybe they even blame me for what happened on Mittend. Set up your portable conference mike, and I'll talk to them."

There was a long pause. Finally, to Steven's complete surprise, a faint smile broke through the severity of that rather heavy countenance. "Steven," said his father finally, "until this minute I'd have sworn that you've stayed alive because of all the protective things I've done for you. But it has just dawned on me that maybe you have an ability to survive in your fashion. All right, I'll respect that. You may remain out here. We shall talk by way of my conference mike. I will try to explain your point of view, though I'm afraid that will not be easy." He broke off. "All right—I'll see you."

He turned and walked into the building.

It was not easy. Boring minutes went by as somebody who was introduced as General Sinter offered objections to Steven's absence. To Steven the argument early became ridiculous, and he several times suppressed an impulse to leave the car and walk off. What kept him was that the general had an almost unbelievable bad habit. It was not at first obvious over the mike-phone system, but presently because of the different voice tones involved, it became obvious. Incredibly, the man carried on two conversations at the same time. One consisted of his dialogue with Steven, principally. The second conversation was a continuing muttering comment on what Steven said and what he himself answered or questioned, whereby his subconscious seemed to be telling what it was thinking.

His opening remark was not too bad, though the

tone was offensive. He said, "Young man, we have already been advised of your claim. So let us just hear you make the statement for the record—I should tell you that this conversation is being taped."

Steven said, "I believe this to be the body of a man named Daniel Utgers. Yet until two days ago I as a self was on Mittend with the rescue expedition. The self that I am talking about has the memory and the feeling of being the identity of Steven Masters, Junior."

Came the undertone comment from the general: "If we were living back in the days of the rack, we'd soon have that story squeezed out of him, and the truth made available."

Next, was the opening statement, "Tell us in your own words exactly what happened."

Steven told his falsehood exactly as he had related it to his father.

The muttered undertone to that was: "Phoniest story I ever heard. Looks like we're going to have to scare the bejesus out of this young S.O.B."

There were more questions and more comments, all equally antagonistic. Yet in an odd, twisted way, the officer seemed, simultaneous with his disbelief, to blame the Daniel Utgers version of Steven for the new disaster on Mittend.

In the end, he cleared his throat, yet his voice was harsh as he said, "I am going to order the arrest of this young man, to be tried by court-martial for conduct and negligence resulting in the death of three officers of the armed forces on Mittend."

Steven addressed his father. "Dad, haven't you had enough of this stupe? I have."

Masters, Senior, spoke to his attorney. His voice as it came over the phone system was calm. "Mr. Glencairn, will you tell these uninformed people what you told me?" To the officers, he said, "Mr. Glencairn is my personal attorney."

Steven recalled Glencairn as a precise-looking individual who wore glasses and had a sharp nose. The lawyer said, "I advised Mr. Masters earlier that by law the body of an individual *is* the person. The body of Steven Masters is, persumably, on Mittend, either alive or dead. If you wish at some future time to place that body on trial in a court, military or civil, you must first bring it back to Earth. I further advised Mr. Masters that Daniel Utgers, whose living body is sitting outside in his car, is a civilian, and cannot be tried in a court-martial by military judges. In the event that the government files charges against Daniel Utgers I shall require a tape of those proceedings. I state now before all of you that in the event the tape is, uh, accidentally destroyed, I shall subpoena the general as a witness. However, before proceeding to such extremes I advise the general to listen to the tape. He seems to have an affliction which, I'm sure, any psychiatrist would be qualified to evaluate. I predict it will be a negative evaluation. Thank you. That is all. I am now advising these two gentlemen, both clients of mine, to leave this area, and I strongly urge that it is illegal for anyone here to prevent such departure. I am sure they accept that they are subject to due process of law. Correct, Mr. Masters?"

"Yes," came the voice of Masters, Senior.

"Correct, Mr. Utgers?" said the attorney.

"Speaking as a body, yes," said Steven over the phone.

Outside, on the street, Masters, Senior, was thoughtful. "That was very unusual behavior," he said finally. "I wonder if General Sinter has been like that before."

The subject did not interest Steven. "Let's go!" he said impatiently over the mike.

"One minute," said his father. He thereupon spoke to the attorney, who had accompanied him from the interrogation room. The two men walked down the street to Glencairn's car, and stood there in earnest conversation for several minutes.

Finally, the elder Masters walked rapidly back to the waiting limousine, climbed in beside Steven, and instructed the chauffer: "Stigmire Towers."

To Steven, he commented, "It's time that we consider the implications of this situation. If you are Steven, then what we have run into on Mittend could be a national danger. So that *all* unusual behavior in relation to you needs to be carefully evaluated."

"Doesn't seem to have affected you. And you would be the biggest catch of all."

His father said nothing to that; but simply leaned back, and they drove in silence the rest of the journey. As Steven climbed out, Masters, Senior, said:

"Since there is already a comparatively large expedition at Mittend, at this moment there is no intention of sending another in the near future. So you will continue to live at the Stig on a limited allowance. I gather your new name and claim will be publicized; so get ready for that. Any message for your mother?"

Tell her I'm better-looking this time, but still not as good as what she produced," said Steven.

Whereupon, he turned and walked off without a backward glance.

CHAPTER 11

✯✯✯✯✯✯✯✯✯✯✯✯✯✯✯✯✯✯✯✯✯✯✯✯✯

Steven awakened in darkness with a memory. He was immediately furious.

That S.O.B. attorney, Glencairn, saying what he did: ". . . The body of Steven Masters is . . . alive or dead—"

It was a thought which, among many others, Steven had never quite allowed himself to experience. Until now.

He turned on the light, and studied his bedside clock, reverse side, where the calendar was. Then he did a little mental addition.

Shock. Blankness. Because—so long. Me. Out there on Mittend, a prisoner, with Mark Broehm at the helm. At the moment of awakening, Steven had somehow got the full effect of the unpleasant implications.

Now, as he became more alert, the disturbed feeling began to abate. Steven, awake, had a hard time worrying about anything.

Nevertheless, after a minute or so, some of the repercussions remained. He got up and went over to the mirror to reassure himself. For at least another minute, then, he stared at the image of Daniel Utgers. And it was not that bad.

Only five years older, he told himself. I can live with that. . . .

He was about to return to bed, when he saw the ghostly figure in the adjacent corner.

Because he could see through it—and instantly noticed that he could—he was not seriously upset. At first. For a moment, in fact, it had the look of one of those minor hallucinations that are the consequence of chance light reflections.

Then the man—it was a man—spoke. "At this distance, in this shadow form," he said in a baritone voice, "I cannot do you damage. But I decided to come and take a look at this latest version of you."

Steven had jumped a little at the first sound of the voice. But other than that he did not move. He was not easily impressed. He could see the wall and part of a chair through the man's body. But he had already had a thought about the method that was being used to produce the effect he saw. In college he had seen laser three-dimensional film and TV. This was a little like that. So he waited, principally wondering who was doing this to him. With that thought—of someone else's purpose—he was abruptly angry. But there was a kind of fear, also.

What shook him now was the realization that he had taken the Browning automatic to bed with him. It was still there, under the pillow.

I'd better try to edge over there. . . . He edged. The intruding image did not try to prevent him.

Steven reached the bed, and brazenly sat down on it.

The man's image stood watching him.

Steven reached over, put his hand under the pillow, and withdrew it, pistol in hand.

The man watched him.

Using both hands, Steven pulled at the rear of the barrel. With a single sliding motion it clicked the trigger into position.

The man who stood opposite the bed near the door, like a wraith, smiled. He was fairly tall, and seemed about forty years of age, well built. He said, "So that's the kind of weapon you produce when in doubt."

Steven rose from the bed, and pointed the automatic. "Who are you?" he demanded belligerently.

The smile grew broader. "That's not an easy question to answer. I'm essentially a stranger in this part of the universe, but I suppose you could say that my place of abode is Mittend. I helped take that planet over from a peculiar cult of good people who long ago attained such a state of mental purity that they can't hurt an insect. They've recently, in the past few years, braced themselves to the realization that they must relearn the art of killing in self-defense, but they really don't know how to do that."

Steven, who had a short attention span, and never listened to explanations, anyway, said, "I haven't the faintest idea what you're talking about."

But he partially lowered his gun.

"All right"—the man smiled—"let me make it simple. When you first landed, that composite being, Mother, saw in you the savior of Mittend. I thought I'd come and take a look to see what she is pinning her hopes on." He shook his head. "Steven, I hate to say this, but you don't look like you're up to the job Mother has in mind for you."

Steven, who had got hung up on an early sentence, asked at that point, baffled, "Save Mother from what?"

"From us Gi-Ints."

"What would I want to do that for?" asked Steven, who had spent most of his life trying to be uninvolved with just about everything.

"I just wanted to make sure that you fully understood the consequences," said the stranger in a genial tone. "So here's your picture: If you, the self, ever come to Mittend again, we Gi-Ints will kill you immediately. Got that?"

Steven had one tiny problem with the meaning. It was a threat. And he didn't like to be threatened. But that was not actually a real difficulty. The truth was, he was not planning to go to Mittend again, ever, if he could help it.

"*Got it?*" insisted the man.

"Just a moment," said Steven.

He had remembered the canister, and his fears about it at the time of his last landing on Mittend. With a sudden movement, and three long strides, he was in the bathroom. "Okay," he called back, "it's a deal."

He had the door closed, then, and he was partly through the other door (which he had to unlock) when there was a violent explosion from somewhere in his bedroom.

The shattering sound of it was ear-splitting. But he kept right on running until he got to the phone in the main living room. From there he called the fire department.

It took about an hour for the firemen to put out the last flickering flame. But Steven didn't stay to see what it looked like. He had a reserve penthouse in another part of the city, and he spent the balance of the night there. He slept soundly.

About noon the next day, he phoned his father. He described what had happened, and then said, "What I'd like is to find out if that blowup was intended to kill me or merely to destroy equipment installed under the floor to produce the three-dimensional image and project the voice."

The elder Masters said, "I've already been over and looked at the damage with some of my engineers. After all, that's a thirty-eight-million-dollar building. The worst damage was in the corner adjacent to the door that leads into the hallway."

"That's where he was standing."

"There was a lot of twisted metal under the floor there," said Masters, Senior.

"That," said Steven with satisfaction, "is what I wanted to know."

"I should inform you," said his father, "that in the opinion of the experts the explosion could have killed you anywhere in the room. Particularly, there seemed to be a lot of flying metal around."

"Good," said Steven. "See you, Dad."

"Hey, wait a minute!" yelled his father.

Steven, on the point of hanging up, reluctantly brought the receiver back to his ear again. "What is it?"

"Several things. First of all, I've asked the police to locate your three servants. Somebody must have come in and installed that machinery while they were in charge."

It was a subject that couldn't have interested Steven less. But he sighed, and waited.

"Now, I have a question," came the voice. "Did a voice in your head warn you?"

"Nope, I just got the hell out of there." Steven had forgotten about his sudden recollection of the canister on Mittend.

"At exactly the right instant, please notice," said his father.

Steven sighed again. He was not interested in a prolonged postmortem. It was done. It worked. Forget it. Next time was another time, to be dealt with then.

"One more thing," continued the elder Masters. "The first of the afternoon papers are on the street. I suggest you have one sent up to your apartment, and read the front-page article about you."

"About the fire?"

"No, that's on page three."

"About Mittend?"

"No. You'll see. Good-bye."

What the paper said was:

NEW MIND-SWAP DEVELOPMENT
Utgers Wife Asks Court Order

Today in court Mrs. Lindy Utgers filed suit in the now-famous mind-swap case, involving Steven Masters.

She alleges that her husband's body belongs to him, and in a legal sense, to her. The district court is being asked to rule that Steven Masters, who claims to be currently in possession of the Utgers body, be restricted from associating with female companions, and restricted from engaging in activities that might cause physical damage to the body or mental distress to her . . .

Steven read the entire article. Then he picked up the phone and called long distance. After a few moments, there was the rather sweet feminine voice.

"Know who this is?" he asked.

Pause, then a suddenly tense voice: "What do you want?"

Steven said, "Looks like we've both got reasons to keep me out of sight and out of circulation. So, why don't you come over here and keep me company until this thing straightens out?"

"Oh, I couldn't do a thing like that. What would my husband think when he comes back?"

"Look," argued Steven. "If he can figure out the moral aspects—if that's what you're referring to—he's a better man than I am."

"From what I've heard about you, everybody is."

"Are you always that quick?" said Steven. He broke off. "Now, listen"—earnestly—"I'm offering you a way out of this dilemma. If you want to know where your husband's body is any time of the day or night, you'd better tell me right now that you're coming. And then you'd better get dressed and drive over here today— by tonight. Speaking of feminine companionship, I can't wait until tomorrow."

There was a tiny moan in his receiver, an indication of anguished doubt at the other end of the line.

"After all," urged Steven, "I've already been with you two days and two nights."

"I didn't know it then," she wailed.

"But *I* did," said Steven. "And so will your husband, eventually." He made his voice calm. "You coming? You not coming? Or do you have in mind waiting to find out whether an Utgers attorney or Masters money can win that court order? Coming, yes or no?"

Long pause. Then a sigh: "Yes."

"Be here before ten P.M." said Steven. "That's my bedtime when I've been single too long."

He hung up, cheerful again. It wasn't that Lindy was so great, or even medium good. A lot of stodginess there. Yet, maybe, now that she knew, she'd speed up a little.

It didn't matter. He, Steven, had nothing better to do for a while.

CHAPTER 12

****

In Steven's first year in high school, when he was still trying, a teacher had said to him: "Steven, why don't you one of these days sit down and just think through all the trouble you've caused since coming into this class?"

It was an unfortunate suggestion. The instant those words were spoken, Steven, first, blanked out whatever else the stupe had to say; and, second, made a total decision *never* to think through things.

Ever since, when a problem or condition was presented to him, he solved it with an instant reaction, or else let it ride by on stream of consciousness association.

Was his reaction correct? That was not a question Steven asked himself. What he did: if there were repercussions, he handled each in turn in the same fashion. If that didn't work, or if he had no answer or association at all, he forgot it.

On the second morning after the explosion, Lindy and Steven moved back to his main apartment. Workmen in relays had repaired the damage. A new bed, and new bedroom furniture had been brought to replace the destroyed items. A team of experts had gone over the apartment, looked for additional bombs, and found none.

That second morning, Steven had a thought. The crux of it, which thereupon instantly became reality, was that the entire Mittend matter needed further looking into by people who did things like that.

With Lindy hovering in the background with the anxious manner of a typical Steven female, he phoned his father, and asked:

"Who made the decision for that expedition to go to Mittend? How long ago was that bomb planted in my bedroom? How come the guy who gave me that Gi-Int malarky spoke in colloquial American? Why did he assume that if a body I'm in is killed, that I won't show up as somebody else I harmed?"

It was such an unexpectedly rational set of questions that the elder Masters was unwary. He had been ardently hoping that these numerous personal threats had finally—as he had worded it to his wife—"brought Steven to his senses." Now, after listening to so many sensible remarks, he falsely deduced that, at last, he could have a logical dialogue with his heir.

What he said was: "I listened very carefully when you first told me about that. My impression is that he kept you diverted so that you didn't have an associated name come into your mind. Perhaps that's the key."

Where he lost Steven, in his comment, was the part about Steven possibly not having noticed something that the older man had. Steven never missed anything. Or, if he did, he forgot that he had.

Steven was now automatically ready to go into the forgetting part. He said, "Okay, Dad. Don't want to take up your time. See you."

"Hey, wa—" began his father.

But Steven had hung up.

When the phone rang again moments later, Lindy had her instructions. "He just went out," she said. "Said he'd be back about midnight."

She was discovering that living with Steven was already different than it had been with Daniel. There was a sense of moving rapidly, even though at this instant Steven himself was lolling comfortably on the settee across the room.

On the phone, Masters, Senior, now expressed astonishment at a female voice answering. "May I ask who you are?"

When she had told him, there was dead silence at the other end. At last: "So Steven is finally married. Give him my best wishes when he, uh, comes home at midnight, and tell him I'll get my staff on that assignment right away."

"I'll tell him," said Lindy.

"And as for you, my dear," said Steven's father, "I'm going to send you, personally, a wedding present approximately the value of the legal fees that I expected to pay to defend him against your suit. You are going to withdraw that, aren't you?"

"I canceled it this morning," she said.

"Good, good, thank you, my dear. Good-bye for now."

After his wife had hung up, Steven said, "The way I look at this situation is, I'm going to stay right here with my little Lindy. Keep the doors locked. And when I go to bed at night, I'll first search the place. Then I'll stay with you so long as I'm awake. At which time we'll tuck you in the spare bedroom. And then—"

He stopped.

Something clanged inside his head.

He was aware of an instant, intense diminishment of his perception. His vision blurred so badly that the deepening darkness merely gave an objective unreality to the subjective distortion which had already made an inner night of what, only seconds before, had been a bright morning. And then—

Another sound in his mind. This one was faint at first, and seemed far away. But it came nearer.

And there were mental images, suddenly. The first picture that came into Steven's conscious awareness was of a man's face. After a moment, he realized it was the same man who had caused the explosion two nights before. The man was smiling in the same ironic fashion.

The sound that had been steady in Steven's mind as the pictures took form became a voice: "Steven, have you ever thought what happens when you do a mind-switch? The processes involved are either impossible—if you'll think about it—or else they're part of some automatic condition in the nature of things.

"That second possibility is the truth. And, because you're connected to the process, you have to be killed —quickly.

"Sorry."

Steven actually didn't hear all that except in retrospect. At the very instant of the man's face becoming identifiable, Steven experienced one of his complex, mostly sub-awareness-level reactions.

He assumed it was a death-threat. He remembered what his father had analyzed. He recalled the Gi-Int making the astonishing statement that Mother wanted him as a savior. He deduced he would have to save himself, because Mother didn't seem to worry if his current body got knifed or bombed.

He did all that without thinking. And then—

His mind flashed over harmed persons. The names that came to contact with his attention were Mark Broehm (on Mittend), Daniel Utgers (on Mittend), the photographer, Apley (who had concealed himself in the bedroom at the time of Stephanie's rebellion), the wild girl (on Mittend). . . .

Steven at once rejected all that. Twice was enough for that uncontrolled crud. His mind thereupon solidly zeroed in on Mother.

For Pete's sake, he thought, if she's connected to me, why don't I get in on *that* deal . . . ? As he had that thought, the man's face began to fade. At the very final instant before it disappeared the face looked astonished, then unbelieving, and then . . . totally ferocious.

CHAPTER 13

✖✗✖✗✖✗✖✗✖✗✖✗✖✗✖✗✖✗✖✗✖✗✖✗✖✗✖

Daniel Utgers awakened in darkness.

He was amazed at himself. He had been, he recalled, reading.

Must have fallen asleep, he chided himself. Actually slipped down to the floor.

What immediately angered him was that Lindy had not come looking for him. The puzzlement aspect of that ended quickly. Because Lindy was like that: mentally a lost soul.

The swift antagonism faded as Utgers realized he was not lying on carpet but on grass. His mind poised in a baffled surmise . . . and the beginning of fear.

He looked up and around at a moonless but starlit sky, with vague shapes nearby on the ground. Two odd-looking buildings (the spaceships) puzzled him briefly. But he gave up on them, as one of the objects lying near him stirred.

His eyes were becoming accustomed to the darkness. now that his inner confusion was clearing up. He was startled to realize that whoever was there was sitting up and had the long hair of a woman.

"Lindy!" Utgers spoke the name with irritation.

Suddenly, it seemed to him that, somehow, his not-too-bright wife had caused what was happening. Exactly how she had done it, or even what she had done, was not clear at this instant. But she was a dimwit with romantic ideas. What he was now seeing and experiencing had elements in it that Lindy, being illogical, could easily have mistaken for the brand of excitement that she craved—and seldom got from an intellectual husband whose hobbies were sports cars and exercise.

Utgers parted his lips to say in a critical tone, "Lindy, for God's sake, what are you up to now?"

Before he could speak the complaint (common in their marriage) an astounding thing happened. The woman climbed shakily to her feet, and staggered off into the night. As she did so, Utgers realized for the first time that she was naked.

"Hey!" he yelled, completely outraged. "Where are you going, you nut?"

The sound of his voice seemed to have a galvanizing effect on the woman. She began to run in earnest. In a few moments she had vanished into the darkness.

Vanished, that is, except for a peculiar misty feeling Utgers had that it was he who was running through the night.

The feeling, the picture of that, receded into a tiny continuing scene at the remote back of his mind as, near him, there was a metallic grinding sound. Though he did not know it, his yelling voice had been heard inside the spaceship. Those inside would now come out and discover the dead bodies. There would be hours of confusion, frank disbelief, anger, outrage, and, finally, uncertainty.

About noon the next day, the second, large module came down from orbit ahead of schedule, with seventeen men aboard, and more equipment. Graves were dug in bitter silence. After a brief service, the dead bodies were lowered into them, and covered up.

For some reason that slightly cleared the emotional atmosphere. Odard actually said gruffly to Utgers, "If such a personality switch did, in fact, occur, where were you when it happened?"

Amazingly, there had been so much tension, that

simple fact had not yet been presented. Utgers said,
"In my library in my home in Westchester, reading."

"What book?" flashed Odard.

"Early Greek Myths, by Denison."

"Oh!" said Odard, sounding dejected.

Since Utgers, aside from being a scion of well-to-do
parents, claimed to be an instructor in ancient history
at Otin College, the book title was all too dully plausible.

After that, there was brief silence between them.
The two men stood there under the bright blue sun
of Mittend. Around them was wilderness that, at casual
glance, did not look too different from Earth. Odard
was only dimly aware of his surroundings. A thought
was struggling for expression from inside him.

"What role," he asked finally, "do you envision for
yourself during the remainder of this expedition?"

"I keep having a picture," said Utgers, "of scenes
that must be from elsewhere on this planet, but near
here. I have a feeling I'm still connected to that girl.
My feeling is that I know where she is and that I can
find her."

"Good God!" said Odard.

The claim of internal connection to another person
settled one thing. Utgers was on the helijet flight that
day. And it was his judgment and feeling that provided the navigator with one false—as it turned out
—direction after another.

The failure actually was in his favor. His companions
grew tolerant, and, in fact, at this point recovered from
a peculiar sense of inferiority in relation to the whole
Steven-Broehm-Utgers mystery.

The second night (the third after the landing) Utgers slept inside the module. All through the night he
was aware of the thoughts and the feelings of the wild
girl, and of beasts swimming in streams, ravenously
seeking the amphibious creatures that dwelt in Mittendian rivers. Seemingly, there were large nonpredatory
animals in the water which he (it seemed as if it were
he) attacked, killed, and devoured.

Utgers woke up shortly after dawn with a disgusted

conviction: I'm a victim of the hallucinations and strange dreams to which this person, Broehm, must be subject. . . .

The analysis reassured him. His sense of personal rightness returned. All that day he tried to ignore the fantasies that he believed came from the disordered brain of Mark Broehm.

It became progressively easier for him to do so.

CHAPTER 14

****

Steven seemed to be in a garden, for there were high walls visible through the greenery.

Lush growth, towering trees, flowers, grass: that was what he saw. Leaves rustling in a breeze, the sound of footsteps on the hard dirt of a pathway, a faint, distant muttering of something—machinery? He couldn't decide what it was he heard. The scent of green things, the rich fragrance of flowers, a kind of permeating wet ground odor: that was what he smelled.

He was a young woman walking in a garden, and he could feel her feet pressing the earth, and the touch of the breeze on her cheeks; and, in the hallucination, inside her head he *knew*.

At first, it seemed as if he knew everything.

Then he realized that he knew only what voices were saying to him, and in his mind's senses he could perceive what those who spoke were looking at, hearing, feeling, touching, and other awarenesses.

Moment by moment some part of him counted the voices. There were $8 \times 11^{23} + 119$. That last figure kept changing at each count. Immediately after 119, it was 1,138. Then it was 821,923. Abruptly, the total jumped to $8 \times 11^{24} + 603$. Next, it came back again to being an 11^{23} number.

Each of the voices had a different message for him. To each message he gave an immediate reply either by projecting the answer back to the speaker with a part of his mind, or providing the individual with the means for accomplishing a request. Or both.

All this cost him no effort and no conscious thought. The multi-multi-multi messages came; he responded to them—whereupon, he did an even more miraculous thing. He had convenient locations within himself—that is, the young female in the garden had those locations—where he (she) filed each message and response for future use, cross-filing in relation to subject, source, words spoken, personnel, scenery, etc., etc., etc., etc.

It was not, Steven began to realize, a "normal" mind-switch. Whoever the "self" of this woman's body had been was gone. That part was par for the system. Presumably, she was now Daniel Utgers, sitting in Stevens Masters' apartment, staring at Lindy Utgers.

What was different was that *this* body and mind continued to function on a level that transcended the entire mental universe of Steven Masters.

In his walk, he now rounded a clump of trees. There, waiting for him, were three young women.

Steven didn't ask himself if they were waiting. He knew it. He came to an immediate full stop.

In a single, encompassing glance, he noticed that all three were good-looking human females, two with blonde and one with brown hair. They were, all three, about five-feet, six-inches in height, and slender of build. They all were dressed in a filmy white, frilly stuff that he had always referred to as "phony angel getup." The "stuff" slopped right down to the ground, and imparted a very pure look to all three wearers.

One of the two blondes said in perfect English, "My name is Eent, Steven. I am one of eight hundred and eight-six women who live in that building over there beyond that clump of trees. Your present body also lives there, and all of us together are Mother."

As she mentioned the building and the number of persons in it, she gestured gracefully with one arm to her left and behind her. If she expected by such a vague pointing movement to turn Steven in that direction, she failed. He started fixedly at her all the time that she spoke. He continued to stare even after she fell silent.

"Then I'm on Mittend," said Steven.

"It's not exactly like that," said Eent. "Our location is not on a planet, really—if you can understand that."

"No," said Steven frankly, "I can't."

"Then don't try," said the brown-haired woman, with a smile. She added, "My name is Ganze. And, Steven, it was very quick of you to reject automatic transference, and to think of Mother. But it's too soon, and I'm sorry to say it won't happen next time you try. So, don't, for your life's sake, take the extra fraction of a second to consider it at some future moment of stress. Moreover, just being in Kalkun's body has changed you, so that you'll never again be switchable into the body of someone you harmed. But despite that improvement, you still have a long way to go before you even get the chance to rescue us."

"From what?" asked Steven.

"Our race attained perfection too soon," said the third woman, and added, "My name is Hormer." She continued, "Too soon, that is, for the way other life is. We had reached a level of inner purity where we could not kill, or do a harmful thing. For many years, now, since we discovered our error, we have been trying to reverse the process, and to learn once more to do what is necessary in the world as it is. To devise a modified approach to violence, and to find a protector who can act forthrightly."

Hormer's was one of those long explanations that usually left Steven blank, and staring unseeing and unhearing at the speaker. Yet he heard a surprisingly large number of Hormer's words. Unfortunately, he got partially hung up on the word "purity."

Purity was not an attractive concept to Steven Masters, Junior, age almost-twenty-three. In his head, purity was dull, sexless, letting other people have their way and not having yours, working hard, going to bed early, reading "good" · books, thinking featureless thoughts, and so on, ad nauseam.

He had always had a single, expressive word for people like that: stupes.

But—no question. While he was here—during the precious moments they were allowing him to "stay" (if he understood correctly, they intended to send him away at any moment)—he was getting information.

Quick, quick, quick, more, was his thought.

He said swiftly, "This building over there—" He pointed where Eent had pointed (to her left and behind), but again he didn't look. "Is it defensible?"

"Not in its proper time," said Hormer. "But, here, away from that whole universe, we are safe."

Steven allowed most of the mind-boggling meaning of that to pass him by, using a simple technique for him: that is, he didn't give it another thought.

"Why not just stay here?" he asked.

They stood there in the bright daylight of the green garden, with a soft breeze blowing their hair and their voluminous frilly, white angelic dresses. All three of them simultaneously shook their heads.

It was Eent who explained: "Out there everything is at a stop. No children are born. The average woman of our race long ago elected to have bred out of her the ability to reproduce, in favor of the concept that only the most perfect genetic females should carry forward the best attributes of intelligent life. Those perfect ones are here in this building, in these grounds. The problem is that the last man we allowed in here to play the role of father was a Gi-Int. Our thought, of course, was that we must add some impurity to the race for it to survive until the rest of intelligent life caught up a little more. Unfortunately, the Gi-Int we selected was destructive in a way that is too long to detail to you. You'll have to evaluate him for yourself. He has twice, now, tried to kill you. That's your problem. *We* left him up there in time. And he's waiting to take us over when we return."

This time so many meanings stimulated in Steven his

one greatest ability. He could select out the wrongness in what people said and did. In that tradition he now rendered one of his instant condemnatory judgments. "For God's sake," he said sarcastically, "how could anybody be so stupid as to have not understood human nature? I began to catch on to stuff like that when I was three years old. And I had my old lady completely under control long before that."

"We," said Hormer, "who can see and feel the energy-flows underneath thought and action, found ourselves feeling compassion for a stopped or twisted flow. But since it seemed to be mechanical we simultaneously underrated the potential danger."

"We looked at a man," said Eent, "and we saw the waves and perceived the light and darkness around him and inside him. Did it matter, we subsequently asked ourselves, what he said or thought when all, or most, of those lines were twisted or stopped? We discovered that, unfortunately, he accepted his own consequent thoughts and feelings as being real even after we pointed out to him that they were not. For a long time, for much too long, we paid no attention to his resistance, thinking that surely he would come to his senses presently. He never did."

"A human being," said Ganze, "is, we observed, like a combination of a solid and liquid. There is continuing outflow and inflow of particles so that, after a little, not one atom is the same as it was before. So to us the problem seemed by this reasoning also to be a matter of physics. But, alas, no matter how often we pointed this out to the individual, the life-feeling that radiated from him retained its previous form. In other words, the identity persisted. He refused to be aware that it's all right to be anybody. But that it's a growth process, and must not be regressive."

"And so," added Hormer, "milllions of such twisted energy-flow types attacked the pure people and murdered them all—except for the few who escaped to Mittend, the nearest Earth-like planet."

There were so many fantastic implications that Steven

tried to encompass them all. But, despite his best effort, a number of the meanings shot past him. A few, it would later turn out, had actually lodged somewhere in his head. It could even be that it all recorded in some hidden location, perhaps in his big toe or the little finger of his right hand. But it was literally true that most of what people had said to Steven during his lifetime had later proved to be unsalvageable, memory-wise.

But what he did register had a distinct dampening effect on him, now. And, as a result—

A grim realization had come to Steven. In finally making it into this secluded garden, his first triumphant feeling had been that here, unexpectedly, was the end of his problem.

It wasn't. They were the defeated. With all their knowledge of, and control of, energy-flows, and atoms, and molecules, and their perception of things microscopic, those whom they had tried to protect had . . . (Something inimical; it wasn't clear what. But not good.)

His thought flashed back to that first time in the biofeedback program. There, he had immediately noticed what apparently neither the individuals, themselves, nor those who dealt with them, had ever considered: that something was as wrong with the doctor as with the patient. The teacher was not exactly crazy, but he had become strange. The observer—the scientist —had failed to observe the effect of the experiment upon himself.

Yet Steven Masters—who at some level of his being was reluctantly aware of what people should be like because he always tried to do the opposite—*he* noticed. And, in that one instance, he had thought about it.

His memory flickered back now to the moment when he had become one female unit of an eight-hundred-and-eighty-six-unit-part of Mother. His impression had been—

A wrongness—that much he remembered.
What?

He temporized while he thought about it, and said, "That father business—you mean, one man for *all* of the women who constitute Mother?"

"All eight hundred and eighty-six," agreed Ganze cheerfully.

"The only thing he has to do," said Eent, "is see to it that each of us produces one child a year."

Steven was astounded. He blinked. Then he did a calculation. "For heaven's sake," he said, "who's going to look after all those kids?"

The three angels just stood there looking at him—and that suddenly struck him.

They're really very beautiful, he thought, almost absentmindedly. It reminded him. His astonishment that first time on Mittend when he saw human beings. "How come," he asked, "you're such normal, handsome white female human beings?"

The three women smiled radiantly. "We're that way for *you*," said Eent. "That's what attracts you. No one sees us the same. Our race is amorphal. But, then, so is yours. But the flows are stopped. The body mass is caught as in a container. The energies reflect back on themselves. Would you like to see me turn into a bird, and fly off?"

"Yes," said Steven.

The way it happened—he was told presently by Hormer—was not for his perception. His eyes twisted. The twist seemed to reach right back into his brain, and he was suddenly dizzy. Involuntarily, he squeezed his lids together. When he abruptly remembered what he was supposed to be seeing, he flicked his eyes open —just in time to see a large swanlike bird make a run across the garden, flapping its wings, and then become airborne. It flew low over the trees.

Steven watched the flight cynically. "I'm unconvinced," he said. "That moment of eye twist had a hypnotic feel to it. Which makes me suspicious. Maybe this whole thing is an hallucination. Human beings turning into swans—"

"Do you suggest," asked Hormer, "that your two spaceflights to Mittend were hallucinations?"

"No."

"Do you believe that your return to Earth, first, as Mark Broehm, and then as Daniel Utgers, were hallucinations?"

"There's something I've been wanting to ask about that," said Steven, remembering. "How come you Mother-women seemed to be connected to those naked people, and how come you sent somebody to kill me several times, and yet now I'm being given all this free information?"

They stared at him, astonished.

"Haven't you realized?" breathed Ganze.

"Oh, my goodness," said Hormer, "don't you know? You're one of the men who's been trained to be the next father. Whoever wins get us all."

"Uh!" said Steven.

For once he was speechless for a reason other than contrariness. Finally: "Wins against *what?*" he gulped.

The words, as he spoke them, had a faraway quality to them. And the garden was suddenly hazy.

"Wait a minute!" Steven yelled—at least he made the mouth motions of yelling that. He heard no sound.

Suddenly, he was in a heavy mist. Yet for a surprisingly long while after he could neither see nor hear, he remained aware of the messages still coming at him from a multi-million points in space, and of the automatic perfection of the answers that replied instantly to each and every incoming signal.

But, presently, that faded, also.

. . . The Utgers body that had been sagging for many minutes on the couch in Steven Masters' apartment stirred. The eyes opened, and gazed up at Lindy, who was anxiously hovering and waiting.

"Where am I?" he muttered.

"You fell asleep," Lindy said sympathetically. "You poor darling! I'll bet having sex six times last night was just too much even for a Steven Masters—"

The bewildered eyes stared up at her. "I don't know what you're talking about," he said. "I'm Mark Broehm." He sat up abruptly. "Hey, I was on that raft, and—and—"

It would take a while.

CHAPTER 15

****

Steven almost fell into the water.

But he was quicker this time. He grabbed with his fingers at two rough rounds of a tree that—he soon discovered—were lashed alongside dozens of similar pieces of wood. Water lapped wetly through and around the numerous uneven cracks.

Safe, he lay puffing as if he had, in fact, been exerting himself. Shock can cause unusual oxygen need. And, because there were more associations in him now, he took a series of lightning surveys of his surroundings.

A wide stream, on either bank of which were the tumbled-down or abandoned buildings of a destroyed city: that was his first swift awareness.

Among those buildings on either shore, he saw no movement, no sign of life.

Gingerly, he edged his body over to the side of the raft, and peered at his reflection.

And so, not more than one minute after the disaster, so rapid were his reactions and sub-awareness thoughts, he was sitting cheerfully on the raft, whistling a little tune under his breath.

It was, he told himself, good to be Steven Masters again. *For real*.

After several minutes of whistling softly, and looking, and thinking, the shore was still drifting by. Or rather—he consciously corrected that subjective awareness—the raft, with him on it, was moving past the shore. Since several minutes was a long time for Steven Masters to be doing nothing, he had, in fact, in his nonthinking fashion, already decided on a tentative long-run goal.

. . . Get over to where the last rocket had come down!

How?

Well, let's get ashore first, he jovially advised the Steven Masters body; in effect, he literally treated the body as separate from Steven, the self. With Steven, that was not a "soul" idea. In Steven's mind, God had died long ago, indeed. He had once in his fleeting way thought of the process of separation of body and self as involving the Kirliann field.

Instantly, that became his explanation for all time. Or at least until somebody bigger and stronger grabbed him by the scruff, and forcibly rubbed his nose in the real truth, whatever that might be, all the time yelling at him what it was. Continued long enough, such tactics had occasionally in the past created an automatic opinion in Steven.

Since no one had taken that much trouble, it was Kirliann all the way. So, no problem, it seemed to Steven. He simply stood up, and was about to dive in and swim to the nearest bank only fifteen feet away —when he happened to glance into the water directly in front of him.

A crocodilelike creature was gazing up at him from a depth of about four feet.

During those first awkward seconds after he sighted the bright red eyes watching him from behind a long snout, Steven was not well. Many simultaneous responses. A fear reflex froze him. Blood drained from the skin into the more central veins and arteries; it was the turning-pale syndrome. Eyes glazed. Muscles lost their tone. Knees felt abysmally weak. During this stage, he sagged down, almost fell, but managed merely to collapse onto the raft bottom.

By the time he could force himself to move and see again, and his body was mobilizing belatedly into the flight reaction, he saw that the thing in the water was swimming after him. The water rippled behind it. The ripple effect was so *long* that Steven now achieved a second, more sustained fear. It was the fear of a person in a canoe who suddenly sees a twenty-foot shark.

That feeling of extreme anxiety was immediately justified. The huge monster lurched toward him, partially surfacing. The great snout came forward through the water like a torpedo. Involuntarily cringing, Steven stepped back, away from that side of the raft.

The poor little craft was not big enough for such a sudden movement. It tilted, his side down, and the side nearest the crocodile up.

Confusion. Steven on one end fought madly for balance. During that moment, the raft reared up and struck the creature a terrific blow under the lower jaw of the long, reaching snout.

There was a great churning. The raft was bobbing wildly, and Steven was on his knees clinging to its far edge with his fingers.

When he finally glanced back, he saw a white glint well down in the water back of the raft. The thought that flashed through Steven's desperate imagination was that the beast had turned over on its back and was now making its approach with its lower jaw as the thrusting, searching weapon which would destroy him.

He had an instant, sinking conviction that this time he wouldn't survive.

In a fleeting fashion he had been glancing ahead and around as these violent events proceeded. As much, that is, as one could glance with eyes that were blurred with fear. But it is a well-known phenomenon that human beings in the presence of a tiger have an automatic tendency to try to claw their way up the nearest tree; so now, quickly, Steven noticed that the stream was getting narrower. He instantly had the hope that he would be able to leap from the raft directly onto the nearest grassy bank.

The stream narrowed. The raft was a dozen feet from the nearest bank. Ten. Nine. He crouched. He gathered his inner forces and readied for a desperate effort. He glanced back again at the monster in the water.

It was climbing up the bank to his left. As it emerged from the water, Steven felt a sudden twisting of his eyes. A moment of blankness. When he could see again, a familiar-looking man was in the act of scrambling to his feet.

The Gi-Int! The man who had twice tried to kill him!

He stood there for a second or two or three, presumably recovering from the transformation. Then he broke into a trot, and was soon running along opposite Steven.

He was naked—which in itself didn't seem too threatening—but a flickering thought in Steven accepted that this creature could obviously transform into any kind of a monster. At the moment he had the same sardonic smile as on both previous occasions. And he called out:

"Steven, you've convinced me. Any man who can use a raft as a weapon—so that for a touch-and-go minute there I almost drowned—has my respect. So why don't you jump over to the bank across from me, and we talk?"

That bank, Steven noticed, was only six feet away. He would have sworn that he could jump it without looking, except that somehow the raft was a little slippery for his boots. So that he skidded and landed in a foot of water, and on his knees. He had to scramble to shore, furious and wet.

Yet, when he got there, and stood up, and turned, the Gi-Int was standing about twenty feet across a rather swiftly flowing stream. And the raft was several score feet farther along. Even as Steven hastily glanced after it, the thing bobbed out of sight behind and beyond some overhanging brush.

He experienced a momentary regret. Despite its crudity it was a vehicle. In his anxiety to get ashore he had forgotten that all the people he had seen here were on foot, and that even a raft had value in such a society.

For Steven—who had his own yacht (which he never used) and his private four-engined jet (with two crews, one on call at all times), and a variety of other transportation at his disposal—somehow, for just the length of time it took to lose it, he had allowed those Earth values to diminish the meaning of a mere raft.

Since having done that made him wrong, he forgot it in the Steven tradition. Instantly, it was as if there had never been such an object. As if his being here on this grassy bank was the real beginning of his present situation. The completeness of the dismissal of the immediate past included such enormous events as how his body had got onto the raft in the first place.

All that had to go, so that Steven would not have to have the thought that perhaps he had made a mistake. And it went. In a flicker of complex repression, it was gone.

With that out of the way, and already feeling more buoyant, he stared over at his enemy, and he said, "What's on your mind, fellow?" His tone, as he asked the question, had the attitude in it: Make your reply quick, and brief.

That was Steven—just about back to normal.

"Steven," said the man across the river, "the way I see your problem and mine is that you've become too powerful for me to dispose of. So you and I have to have an agreement."

The statement left Steven blank. At the moment he had nothing to defend himself with but his personality and a rather tattered spacesuit. Not one weapon. Not even a knife or a food supplement was in any of the pockets of that suit. In emerging from the first spaceship that first day on Mittend, he had scorned having anything in his pocket which would detract from his figure.

It had been said of Steven by a witty friend (who ceased to be a friend as of the moment of the remark) that if the law of averages ever caught up with Steven, and he got what he deserved, he would disappear in a single puff of ego.

There was a more peculiar truth to the observation than its originator realized. Steven *was* ego incarnate, and that was it. He did not lie, or pretend. Steven was not a person who *sought* to gain an advantage by conscious skulduggery. The falseness in him was exactly that: *in* him. He was a solidly woven fabric, so to say, operating entirely on instant forgetfulness, a philosophy of you-have-to-handle-the-world-the-way-it-is, and self-delusion.

Now he stared at the other man, baffled, and said, "I don't know what you mean—powerful. All I've got right now is my bare hands. And maybe I can find a heavy stick that I can use as a club."

For that, he got the same sardonic smile. Whereupon, on his side of the waterway, the naked human-looking being sank down on the grass, and said in a relaxed voice, "Steven, my name is Kroog, and I'm about four thousand Earth years old, and I'd like to convince you that in the long run you can't win against me."

Steven sighed. "I thought we settled all that back on Earth," he said, "that first time you came to see me. And then—after I agreed—you tried to kill me. So what's your next lie?"

"If I thought I could kill you easily," said Kroog, "I'd be over on your side of this stream, change myself into a beast like a bear or a lion, and tear you to bits. You say you have no ordinary defenses like one of those little guns. I believe you." He shook his head. "No, Steven, that's not our problem. You're a father-trainee, and I have the distinct impression that you're

the one Mother wants to win. What I want you to promise is that you're not even going to try."

"Okay," said Steven, "provided you get me back to
Earth."

"I'm not accustomed," said Kroog, and he seemed
baffled now, "to such instant agreements."

Steven said, "Look, I've got all the women I'll ever
need."

"You don't understand," argued the other man.
"This is a special situation. Every year these women
turn out eight hundred and eighty-six kids for you."

"Too many people in the world already," dismissed
Steven. "And, besides, who'd look after them?"

"Are you kidding?" said Kroog. "Mother gets the
wealth of about ninety-eight thousand planets chan-
neled over to her. That includes servants by the tens
of thousands, and whole sections of a planet here or
there set aside for her offspring."

"For Pete's sake," said an amazed Steven, "how did
somebody like me from a little planet like Earth draw
a lot in a game like that?"

"Because Mother, all those mothers, are originally
from Earth. Like they told you, there in that part of
Greece the race got perfected accidentally. Then they
discovered they were at everybody's mercy. About four
thousand years ago a spaceship was built and the
survivors flew off to Mittend."

"I suppose," said a skeptical Steven, "out there in
Greece is also where you learned to speak colloquial
English."

"I personally," said Kroog, "am not from Earth. I just
hooked in onto this deal for twenty years before
Mother realized that my offspring were worse than
me. Most Gi-Ints go back to Earth periodically. The
last time I lived for over twenty years in New York."

Steven said, "I suppose Gi-Ints has a special meaning."

"You saw me in the water?"

"Sort of a crocodile," said Steven, frowning.

"In order to take over those eight hundred and

eighty-six human women," said Kroog, "I had to adjust myself to the Earth biological patterns. Now I can only transform to Earth-originated people and beasts." There was suddenly a change in his voice. New color came into his face. His eyes brightened. He breathed faster. "Steven, if you ever want to know what real excitement is, try the volatile emotional ups and downs and total savagery of a carnivorous animal."

Steven shrugged. "Okay, you do that when you feel like it. Then you become human again. Compares to an average guy having sex before breakfast. After that, he gets out of bed and goes down to work. It's out of his system for a while."

"Unfortunately," said Kroog, suddenly grim, "there's been an unexpected feedback to the savagery and ferocity of the more primitive beasts. As a human, I have many times attacked and bitten to death other human beings. Particularly, I've done this with women after the sex act. Then I devour the tasty parts."

"Which are?" asked Steven.

Kroog seemed not to hear. "What Mother wants," he said, "is a man who will give up his own identity—a total abandonment of the ego idea. That's just about the opposite of where we Gi-Ints are heading, genetic-wise."

"Sort of the old merging-with-the-race idea." Super-egotist Steven shuddered. "Eastern philosophy stuff."

"That's it," said Kroog.

"Ugh!" said Steven.

If he had needed anything to convince himself that Mother could go peddle her charms to someone else— that did it.

Steven said, "Okay, no further comment. What now? Have we got a deal?"

"You're still not interested?"

"In what?" said Steven.

There was a pause on the other side of the river. People on Earth often fell silent after they had talked to Steven for a while.

The man said at last, slowly, "I'm beginning to see

the bent of your mind. Maybe I should have noticed that before. All right, I will take you to Earth, myself, in my own ship."

"Let's go," said Steven.

"Aren't you curious about what destroyed this city?" Kroog asked plaintively.

"I never did go in for ruins on Earth," said Steven. "Why should I be interested in them here?"

Kroog said, "My kids take turns firing heavy Earth artillery at it every night. That's to make sure Mother doesn't get to thinking maybe she can wave her magic wand and rehabilitate the place."

Steven was staring off into the distance. The explanation, if that was what it was, had passed him by.

The naked man sat for a while on the grass. Then he stood up with a decisive motion. "Okay," he said, "let's go."

CHAPTER 16

★★★★★★★★★★★★★★★★★★★★★★★★★

During the journey home in a spaceship that looked like a small jet with stubby wings, Kroog made only one remark that puzzled Steven. The Gi-Int said to him after they had eaten their first meal, "Did you feel anything just then?"

"No." Puzzled but true.

"The ship just went through its time adjustment. So we're back in your normal time." He seemed to take it for granted that Steven would understand.

Steven said, "When do we land?"

"After we eat one more meal."

If so, it was about ninety times as fast as the trans-light speed-system of Earth ships.

It was so.

The craft settled down toward a building, the roof of which folded in upon itself at the last minute to admit them, then folded back into position when they were inside. It was a dark night, and Steven's impression was of open countryside and perhaps a barnlike structure.

He was not really interested. So, after they climbed out of the ship, he followed Kroog through a door along several corridors, and then through another door into a garage. Kroog climbed behind the wheel of what, when he turned the headlights on, was revealed to be a green Mercury. At his beckoning motion, Steven also got in the front seat.

The garage door opened, and they drove out, and off along what seemed to be a country road. They drove for about an hour through country that looked vaguely like New Jersey. Then they came to an airport. The sign said: AIRPORT—*Patterson, Penna.*

Kroog drove up to the bright entrance, took out a billfold, and counted out two hundred dollars in twenty-dollar bills, and gave the money to Steven. "You'll need this to get to New York."

Steven said, "Okay."

He was about to open the door and get out, when Kroog made the statement that explained his total adherence to the promise he had made.

"I analyze," he said, "that it's to my interest to trust once in your attitude to this whole business. After all, if you pursue the matter further, we're merely back where we started. So all I can say is, if you show up again on Mittend, have your guns ready, and be prepared to die."

Steven was ever so slightly irked by the comment. A threat of any kind unbalanced something deep inside him.

In this instance, the unbalancing was not sufficient to justify the discomfort of another journey to Mittend. "Don't worry!" he said irritably. "You'll never see me again, if I can help it."

He thereupon got out of the car, seething a little. He walked straight into the waiting room without a backward glance. Presumably, Kroog drove off, but that could never be provable by Steven. For him, there was the tiresome business of standing in line, and buying a ticket for a heli-taxi, due to leave for New York in thirty-eight minutes. Before boarding, Steven, who had been having those instant reaction thoughts about the repercussions of his homecoming, phoned his father.

When the familiar voice came on, Steven began at once. "Listen, Dad, I'm back, as me this time, and—"

That was as far as he got. There was a gasp at
the other end. And then, a faltering voice interrupted,
saying, "Steven, it's you—"

For Pete's sake, thought Steven, of course it's me.
I just told him it was, and if he's got ears he can also
recognize my voice. . . .

He was about to utter these sentiments, when, to
his complete amazement, the old S.O.B. said again,
"Steven, it's you," and burst into tears.

It took a while before Masters, Senior, was coherent
again. During that while Steven kept glancing impatiently at his watch. Actually, he had plenty of time.
But he had an inner feeling that, in fact, any time
spent talking or listening to his father was a waste.

When the emotional coast was finally, reasonably,
clear, Steven said, "I don't think I should have to run
into the Utgers business. So, how about you sending
somebody over to my apartment and kicking those two
out of it before I make my entrance. Okay?"

"We'd better question Utgers first," said Steven's
father, whose marbles had by this time rolled back
into his head. "I deduce it's Mark Broehm, and we
should get his story."

"You question him," said Steven.

"Okay, okay." The elder Masters spoke hastily.
This was a Steven he knew. It was the old attitude
of uninvolvement back, evidently, in force. "I'll have my
secretary send you a transcript."

Steven parted his lips to say, "Don't bother!" Then,
he closed them, tolerantly. He was remembering his
long-time policy of letting the old buzzard go through
certain harmless motions. The old fellow, who was
by now an incredibly ancient forty-four-years old, had
early started the habit of keeping Steven "informed."
As a consequence, there was a filing cabinet in one
of Steven's clothes closets that probably contained a
summary of the entire Masters worldwide business
operation—of which Steven had never read a line.

There was a throat-clearing sound on the line that
warned Steven of more dull remarks on the way. Steven

cut them off with an instant lie: "My plane, Dad. Got to go. See you!"

"Good-bye," said his father in a resigned tone.

" 'Bye," sang Steven.

He hung up, relieved to have got that chore done.

Approximately thirty-one minutes of flight time later, the hover-craft settled down on the roof of Stigmire Towers, and unloaded a medium tall, extremely tanned youth. Steven at twenty-three could pass for eighteen, except for his eyes, and they were not clearly visible in the artificial lights of the rooftop.

Since his was the penthouse apartment he walked briskly across to the building roof entrance, walked down one flight of steps, and there was the door.

Well, thought Steven, suddenly feeling cheerful. It's back to the good-old-Stig-days for me again.

The affirmation made, he opened the combination lock, turned the knob, and entered.

Immediately inside the front entrance was an alcove. It was so designed that people coming in could not instantly see who was in the great living room beyond.

As Steven stepped into the broad alcove, with its cloak room and such, he saw that the lights in the main room were on.

Oh, for God's sake, he thought, the old so-and-so is here.

Thinking, Damn it, couldn't even leave a guy alone until morning, he walked in; and the first person (and, as it turned out, the only person) he saw was Lindy Utgers.

She was sitting on the couch facing the alcove door, her long legs scrunched under her. Her face was scarlet but determined.

Steven walked over, and looked down at her. He said, "You here alone?"

Lindy nodded. Then she swallowed. Then she said in a low voice, "Mark left when your father sent a car for him." She added, with a shrug, "I refused to go."

"What about that original plan to protect the body of Daniel Utgers from other females?" asked Steven.

Lindy stared past him. Her color remained high. "It doesn't seem important," she said finally. "After all, it wouldn't really be Dan. I can see the difference now."

"I'm not Dan either."

"I'm used to you," Lindy said brightly, "as a personality." She added, "After one hour of realizing that Mark was really Mark and not you, I just went into your bedroom and locked the door. And I stayed there until the phone rang, and it was your father."

Hers was the typical old-style female reaction (Steven believed in his belittling way) to the Masters fortune. However, fact was, her loyalty on this first night of his return was all right with him. He sensed that the Steven body had been deprived of female companionship. He had already been wondering who among his former girlfriends he could phone.

Now that wouldn't be necessary. Good old Lindy would fill in the empty spaces during the next few days, while he gathered his life back into one piece.

Steven had a vague, unhappy conviction that there would be unavoidable interruptions and interrogations. And so, yes, until all that crud was done with, Lindy—despite her age, for twenty-six suddenly seemed far gone to Steven—would, nevertheless, do.

Alas, it wasn't going to be that simple.

CHAPTER 17

****

Steven started low on any sanity scale.

But he was never, after a certain age, scattered. No schizo, Steven. If there was a simple psychiatric classification that fitted him, it was—paranoid.

Take a narrow view of the universe, add extra subjectiveness and delusions of grandeur . . . Steven.

Steven in somebody else's body was not another personality. He was Steven all the way.

That is, until his return from Mittend.

Persons who observed Steven during the days after Lindy Utgers became his daily, and nightly, companion reported odd lapses in him.

He had a tendency to go into brown studies. He would be sitting, or standing—and, suddenly, it was as if a transfixing association took him off into an inner universe.

Was it—could it possibly be—that a psychic switchover was taking place inside that handsome skull to the extreme withdrawal of schizophrenia? The people in Steven's circle who knew about things like that, and who began to flock to his nightly parties as in the past, whispered this question to each other. The answer was nearly always yes.

Actually, it would be difficult even for the most learned member of the psychiatric profession to do more than speculate about a survival type like Steven.

Unknown to those around him, Steven was having second thoughts about Mother.

(It was a subject about which he had told no one. So naturally they couldn't possibly have any idea what was going on during those lengthening moments when he went into a state that had something of the look of suspended animation.)

Steven's own attitude was highly self-critical. He hurled epithets like *ridiculous, stupid, meaningless,* and *absolutely impossible* at each attention lapse. But the phenomenon went on, and on.

What Steven was really manifesting is that you can't be automatic all your life. And then, when the chips are down, not continue to be automatic.

It has been shrewdly observed that the male of the human species has a strong inclination to want to spread his seed. On the one hand, he is secretly a godlike being —the comparable attribute in a woman is being a secret princess. On the other hand, he lives in a world in which people can't shut up, yet have a need, simultaneously, to be negative in what they say. Hence, the individual is eagerly told at some early age that his destiny is to be eaten by worms.

That spoils everything. Thereafter, his normal impulse is to be immortal through children. Of course, Steven, who started being contrary before puberty, had from the suspicious beginning of his assault on females made absolutely sure that one of them didn't sneak a pregnancy over on him.

All of Steven's conscious cogitation pursued that same dismissal of Mother's purpose: Ridiculous, stupid, not worth a minute of time . . . but the associations kept surfacing. Scenes, images, female figures in angelic white, imaginings about, by, in, on, for, to, etc., having 886 children a year.

There was also another memory: what Kroog had said about being over four thousand years old. At the time that colossal number had passed Steven by. But it had got snagged by an observant part of him. And he held it up periodically before his mind's eye, and stared at it in absolute amazement.

So, the two automatic motivations moved along side by side in his head, and refused to lie down and die when sternly ordered to do so by Steven.

As it turned out, he didn't really have too much time to think about it.

CHAPTER 18

★★★★★★★★★★★★★★★★★★★★★★★★★★★

"You sonofabitch!" screamed the sergeant. "When I call you, Masters, *you come*. On the double."

Steven, who had started running at the first sound of his name, already on this eighth morning of his life-term had a clear picture of the nature of military-prison procedure.

"Yes, sir," he said now, breathlessly. He saluted smartly, and tried to balance himself into a semblance of attention. It was hard to do because he was trembling from his exertion. "What is it, sir?" he puffed.

"Pick up my pencil! I dropped it."

"Very well, sir."

Steven thereupon sprang forward, snapped down to his knees, picked up the pencil where it lay in front of the other's desk, scrambled to his feet and to attention, and said, "Shall I give it to you, sir? Or place it on your desk, sir?"

The gray-blue gaze of the heavyset noncom deliberately sought Steven's blue eyes, found them, and demanded subservience. Steven gave it at once by refusing to lock glances.

The noncom, who was about thirty, and whose name was Emmett Obdan, said, "Place it on my desk between my hand and the sheet of paper lying in front of me."

Doing so required Steven to lean across the desk. He immediately deduced what was coming. He braced himself, stepped forward, leaned forward, and reached. As he finished placing the pencil, the sergeant's hand flicked up. The flat palm slapped Steven sharply across the cheek.

Steven jerked back, came to attention, saluted, and said shakily, "Thank you, sir."

The human mask in front of him snarled, "Get back to your cleanup job, and don't give me any more of your lip!"

"Yes, sir."

Steven saluted again, spun around sharply, and started his run across the compound.

From behind him came a shriek: "Masters, get back here!"

Steven slid to a halt, whirled, and returned to the desk at his deadest run. The same salute procedure, and then, breathlessly, "Yes, sir? What is it, sir?"

The sneering eyes stared up at him for a minute. Then: "There's something about your reaction to my training methods, Masters, that I don't like."

"I thought I was fitting in perfectly, sir," said Steven.

Obdan seemed not to hear. "I keep having the impression, Masters, that you hate my guts. That, in short, you're reacting emotionally against me as a person for the realities of military-prison discipline."

"Oh, no, sir, I appreciate your objective approach."

Again, the heavyset man ignored his comment. "Masters, we cannot allow outward conformance and inward resistance. As a preliminary for that part of your training, get down on your knees and lick my boots!"

There was a pause.

"Well?" Scream. *"What are you waiting for?"*

Steven licked dry lips. "I'm afraid, sir, if I do as you ask, you'll kick me in the face."

"So?" Screech.

"You might do me severe damage, sir," said Steven.

"So?"

"I'm afraid people would notice, and punish you for it, sir."

Obdan went into an elaborate act of surprise. He let his mouth fall open. His eyebrows went up. He glared. Finally: "Well, I'll be damned. Concern for *my* welfare. That's very touching, Masters. But you're not the first on that. There must be something basically lovable about me, Masters. Because just about every one of the slackers like you sooner or later gets that very feeling, and—"

It was one of those long verbalizations, the kind that, no matter what the subject or how personal, Steven had never been able to follow. As the mad voice raved on, unheard, its maniacal message shooting by him at the speed of sound, it was for Steven a strangely clear moment (except for the screeched words). He was aware of the other prisoners on the other side of the compound vigorously scrubbing away. Until a few moments ago he had been working beside them. And then, suddenly, this! His fifty-third nightmare in eight days. That was the number of confrontations Obdan had forced on him, starting the first morning at 6 A.M.

Each had been accompanied by one or more slaps, one or more kicks in the shins, and so that close-to-the-surface impulse in Steven to lash back was held in only by one grim fact. There were armed guards on the other side of steel bars, mere yards away. Each time Obdan did his thing, the three nearest unlimbered their rifles, and stood at the ready.

Would they really shoot to kill? Steven was almost at the point where he was willing to make the test. But not quite.

Standing there, he let his gaze stray toward the bars. Just a quick check to see if the rifles were there. At once, his heart sank. There were four of them. They already had their rifles waiting, and they were watching.

Okay, okay, he thought, I guess I'm doomed. . . .

Everything had descended on him at almost the same speed as what was now transpiring. By the second morning, the military had him over at the biofeedback lab, to be debriefed, as it was called.

It was an enforced condition. But he didn't have to

like it. And, being Steven, he had no particular ability to suppress his hostility. So he made an enemy.

To Steven, it seemed obvious that the biofeedback people didn't know what they were doing. Experimenters got sick, and nobody noticed *that*. Their tongues loosened, and they gabbled incessantly—and those who were like that didn't connect the reaction with their work.

He could hardly hear the new man—Bronson—who was assigned to interrogate him. Bronson's voice kept fading to a whisper, and occasionally, when it was very bad, he would wave an arm vaguely, and mutter, "I'm like that. It's nothing."

Bronson wanted a complete account of, as he meticulously worded it, "what you say happened to you here and on Mittend."

That particular way of referring to his experiences got to be pretty irritating to Steven. On the second day, after he had been led in detail through more tiresome recounting of the same facts, Steven finally sat up and made his first attempt to get some information on his own.

"Let's accept for a moment," Steven began, in a tone of voice that he tried to keep even and unhostile, "that what I say happened on Mittend, actually did happen."

Bronson's bright brown eyes narrowed. "It is not my job," he said, "to make (something)." The word could have been "evaluations," but unfortunately his voice had started to fade as he began speaking, and the sound cut down from audibility to inaudibility on a steep curve.

Steven persisted. "If," he said, "there is such a thing as shape-changing, why didn't that Gi-Int shift over to some earlier Earth life-form like one of those prehistoric monsters, or why didn't he take on some completely alien form such as, I presume, exists on one of those 98,000 planets that Mother is connected to? In a getup like that, he could have demolished me with one swish of a dinosaur tail."

Steven gained a benefit from his question for a reason

that he never knew. When a skeptic is presented with the exact doubt that he is having difficulty to restrain himself from expressing, when, moreover, the doubt is uttered by the person who, until that moment, is suspected of being a swindling liar (Bronson's view of Steven's whole story), then for another moment there is confusion. And, ever so briefly, truth.

Bronson said, "It's doubtful if anything but a shadowy memory remains in the cells, of man's ancient-sea or early-monster origin. Therefore, the programming available—that is, the blueprint—could not be duplicated. But the ability to duplicate a crocodile presumably could be achieved by direct interaction between the two Kirliann fields." Bronson shrugged. "I wouldn't know why the same duplication could not be achieved with an alien."

It was an honest reply. It had been evoked by an accidental trick of human psychology. It was partly muttered, partly whispered, partly breathed, partly hissed, but most of it came through. It earned for the man Steven's first reluctant accolade. Which belatedly reminded Steven of what somebody had once urged on him: that a psychiatrist does not have to be sane himself in order to cure people. If he knows his discipline, and adheres to it, he can fix up someone else's marriage though his own is crashing about his ears, etc. Similarly, Bronson could use the complex EEG system, manipulate the Kirliann fields, activate the stimulators, and do a mechanically perfect debriefing.

Unfortunately, it was a little late for Steven to have his first favorable impression. Even more damaging, in an adjoining room an expert had the Utgers version of Mark Broehm recounting *his* experiences.

What Steven didn't know, and what the interrogators at first had difficulty rationalizing, was that Mark said he had been on Mittend only five days. The comparable time that had gone by for Steven was two months and eleven days.

That was a lot of minutes and seconds.

After his interrogation the third morning, as Steven

was about to enter the huge lab-complex commissary for lunch, he was arrested and taken to a military prison.

At the trial, which began only two days later before five generals, the charge was that he had never, personally, gone to Mittend. As the prosecutor put it in his opening remarks: "We wish respectfully to call to the attention of this court that the accused is a man whose father's influence deprived the military of an opportunity to reeducate a spoiled rascal."

He continued, "It is widely known that the superwealthy and the super-powerful often spend money to locate look-alikes, and then utilize their services for a wide variety of dangerous activities.

"The substitute Steven was obviously offered enough money, and he subsequently flew off to Mittend. Arriving there, he failed to take normal precautions (probably because he wasn't the real person, and so did not take the voyage seriously). What he did is well known. He wandered off, and probably got himself killed."

When Bronson got on the stand, the tone of serious invalidation changed to one of total ridicule. He refused to present any documentation. The biofeedback system, he said, operated partly on a basis of sincere cooperation. He added, "I knew we were in trouble when Steven asserted that he had flown back from Mittend in a day or two in a super-spaceship operated by an ex-crocodile."

It was Glencairn's opinion afterward that Steven never had a chance after that line was spoken.

The attempt by the defense attorney to have Bronson's testimony documented was overruled. The prosecutor's subsequent objections to any defense evidence or defense witness were sustained so consistently that, finally, Glencairn said with a wry smile:

"I should like to commend the prosecuting colonel for his remarkable understanding of the prevailing weather conditions in this court. It's winter time for Steven Masters, Junior."

. . . To Steven, poised there in prison in front of

Sergeant Obdan, those memories didn't exactly flit through his conscious mind in sequence. But they were in him in a single, large, anguished lump.

"Get down," spat Obdan, "or I'll come around there, and really—"

As those words spewed forth, Steven Masters was at last squeezing up those momentary sub-awareness reactions that constituted his brand of logic at a time of extreme stress.

A memory: Can't become Mother!

A memory: Can't become someone he had harmed. . . .

(He had been told those two realities, and he believed them.)

Who, then?

The split-second reaction was that it had to be someone he had been kind to.

He couldn't think of a single such person, except, maybe—no, that was too marginal. Besides— no . . . !

At that ultimate instant, the thought came close enough to Steven's consciousness so that he was revolted at the possibility of precipitating anyone into his predicament.

"No, no!" Steven almost yelled.

"Yes, yes!" mimicked the noncom, surging to his feet.

But the fact was he was no longer talking to Steven.

CHAPTER 19

★★★★★★★★★★★★★★★★★★★★★★★★★★

Steven lay for a while with eyes closed, experiencing an absolutely devastating new emotion. He hated himself.

Because he guessed who he was.

And, of course, at this hour of the morning, at a few minutes after eight, he took it for granted that Stephanie either would be in her own or somebody's bed . . . with somebody.

The prospect that there might be a man in bed with Stephanie did not evoke from Steven the hope, Oh, boy, now I'll get a chance to feel what sex is like from the other side. . . .

In a flash of instantaneous anxiety, Steven became a potential Lesbian—the male role.

But his thought and feeling had been snatched and diverted by the mere idea of such a thing. For a minute or so he forgot the rest.

Tense, he opened his eyes. Shuddering, he turned his head, and saw—

He (she) was alone.

Well, thought Steven, relieved, and already tolerantly condescending, maybe, after all, she's really just another good girl waiting to get married.

In his swift look, he'd had a partial glimpse of a spread of gorgeous blonde hair, neatly stretched across to the next pillow. Since he suspected at once that the hair was now his, he cringed with a masculine shame at the awful degradation of having been demoted to the status of being a woman.

A number of small seconds went by. And then—a realization with an impact: It doesn't really feel any worse. . . .

Good God!

He was a body with a head and a brain. The tiny difference of the genitals and their connections throughout the system did not seem to be intruding on his awareness.

With that, so rapid was the adjustment, he literally didn't give it another thought.

Whereupon, memory returned.

Instant visualization of poor little Stephanie confronting Sergeant Emmett Obdan.

Out of bed. Sitting up. Grabbing for the phone.

He had glimpses as he did so of an extremely feminine night dress, a gleam of exposed ivory-white leg, a slender hand holding the receiver, and fine, slim woman's fingers dialing the secret number.

It was somehow a little harder to convince Steven Masters, Senior, this time. The convincer was not quite the same positive-type Steven—after fifty-three one-sided bouts with Sergeant Obdan. But approximately one hour after the call, the elder Masters, accompanied by two woman secretaries, entered Stephanie's apartment.

The two secretaries went out into the kitchen and made themselves some coffee. Steven Senior and Steven Junior sat in the living room.

Steven's father listened with a faraway expression as Stephanie's slightly husky voice, with its occasional breakthrough of engaging soprano overtones, described Steven's first eight days in jail.

Steven concluded with a genuine expression of surprise at the rough treatment he had received. He'd had —he reported truthfully—critical but casually pure thoughts about the armed forces in all its aspects. His companions on the two expeditions to Mittend were typically brave officers, honest, determined, and dedicated. Even his sentence to life imprisonment with hard labor had at the time of the sentencing seemed one of those cruddy but simplistic fates that happened to people when they got down to the stupe level. "Which," Steven concluded, "is what I was after I volunteered for that first expedition."

"It's hard for me to believe," said his father, after a silence, "that you didn't cause some problems in prison, and so earned somebody's instant dislike."

"We were all lined up," said Steven, "and this character Obdan came along, and did something to fourteen out of twenty-three men. By the time he came to me, I had the picture, and I was standing stiffly at attention. But he hauled off and gave me a terrific slap in the face. It was so hard it nearly knocked me down. Then he was outraged that I was no longer at attention, and kicked me in the shins. That was a few minutes after six A.M. the first day."

Stephanie's slender body shrugged. "After that, I just thought I'd better fit in while you and Glencairn did what you could out here."

"We've run up against a stone wall," said his father soberly. "Apparently, the climate inside that military court reflected the sentiment of people in general. You've been publicized as an irresponsible playboy, and you're being held to blame for the death of those three men on Mittend. So, no one dares do anything, for fear it will appear as if they've been bought by Masters money."

Steven had his first *reaction*, that peculiar complex of sub-awareness thoughts that constituted his only claim to being able to think logically. "That sounds as if I, personally, am a target, and I can't believe that."

"It was an excessively rapid trial," his father said in a cautious tone.

Stephanie's silvery voice projected: "If my name is mud, maybe in your defense of the Broehm version of Utgers you can get the documentation they wouldn't allow in the military court."

"That was our plan," was the reply, "but suddenly the case against him was dropped. He's free."

Steven said, "That compound Mother out there somewhere implied that they've been fighting the Gi-Int invasion for many years, and that one of the things that made resistance possible at all was that there's some kind of internal adjustment that's very difficult when you're trying to transfer from one galaxy to another. For that, the Gi-Int needed models."

The elder Masters said, "Mittend was selected as a target for an interstellar expedition because it was a planet that suddenly appeared in orbit around a star without previously detected planetary bodies. The person who made the decision to go there was General Sinter."

Steven's reaction: "The real Sinter is probably in an unmarked grave somewhere."

"Or was eaten," said the older man in an even voice.

"Good God!" said Steven.

"I've been looking at star maps," said Masters, Senior. "The solar system is right here at one upper edge of our galactic wheel, with virtually empty space between us and any of the galaxies in that direction."

"Still," argued Steven, almost as if he were really thinking in a sustained fashion, "there can't be too many advance Gi-Int agents like Kroog and Sinter. Or they wouldn't have felt it necessary to use somebody like me as a diversion."

"You don't sound like a diversion," said the old man grimly. "And that's what I don't understand. What do you know that would require someone to make a total effort to get you out of the way?"

Steven was silent. He was remembering something he had told no one: the 886 females out there who had him targeted as a potential mate.

As that uneasy memory touched him, he felt . . . a shadow.

Deep inside him was a continuing connection with Mother. Some part of him counted all those messages with her, and responded to all of them minute by minute . . . with her.

Instantly, he had a thought: those thousand people he had harmed were an answer.

The proposition he heard himself making to his father was that Masters money be used to buy everybody off.

The elder Masters said, astonished, "How will you remember all the names sufficiently well for us to be able to locate them?"

That was an awkward moment. How explain that he had kept track of all the S.O.B.'s?

After considering the pros and cons on that for his usual one-tenth of one-quarter of a second, Steven said, "We'd better get over to the Stig, and I'll show you." He had a thought. "Is Lindy still there?"

"No," said his father. "I gave her the entire amount of money it cost her husband to defend himself from your harassment, and she went home." The great man smiled. "She called me later, and it seems her return home turned out lucky. The Mittend expedition made one of its periodic contacts with families; and so she talked to the Mark Broehm version of Daniel Utgers, told him about the money I gave her, whereupon he asked her to thank me. So that fits in with what you're suggesting."

"What bothers me," said Steven, "is how come they haven't got to you?"

"I'm like you," said Steven Masters, Senior. "I'm a survival type. And I'm always under guard in a very complex way. It would require a very big organization to penetrate my system. Frankly I don't have the impression that they're that big yet on Earth."

CHAPTER 20

★★★★★★★★★★★★★★★★★★★★★★★★★★

That afternoon a stenographer came to the Stigmire apartment and typed all the names from Steven's handwritten records. Copies were made. A large detective firm placed its entire staff on the job—and after a while the phones began to ring.

The searchers located nine hundred and twenty-three of the slightly more than one thousand names on the list, and they did it in slightly over two days. The elder Masters, who came in periodically and monitored what was happening, shook his head in amazement at the number of persons.

"I don't see how you had the time to harm that many individuals, and you only twenty-three now."

"It wasn't easy," muttered Steven.

He was a little amazed, himself. Boy, what a waste that had been. Yet, he had, he realized, always got a special pleasure out of over-evening the score with people who committed minor offenses against him, or who he imagined had done so.

Now, all that had to be rectified. False or true, peace would have to be declared, or purchased. Since the "harm" thing was the Big Idea with Steven Masters, Senior, the cash for payment was available.

Girls with pleasant, musical voices phoned the men on the lists. Men with pleasant, masculine (meaning baritone) voices phoned the women.

The story that had been decided on was tried and true. Steven, it was said, had got religion as a result of his imprisonment. He now regretted his pranks, his unkind acts. Was there some way in which he could make amends?

A hall was hired. A meeting time was scheduled. Only a handful of individuals said, in effect, "Tell Steven to go to hell. He can't pay me enough money for what he did to me."

All the rest were evidently stimulated by the possibility that maybe he could.

A special corps of negotiators were sent out to argue with the holdouts.

On the night of the meeting, the audience began to arrive early. It had been assumed on the basis of many inquiries that a majority of those attending would bring their spouses, and that turned out to be essentially true.

The entrance was bugged, and so amplifiers in remote listening and watching rooms picked up some interesting conversations.

A husband to his wife, in a protesting voice: "But I still would like to know, how did you ever meet this character, Steven Masters? And what did he do to you that harmed you?"

"Now, dear," his wife said impatiently, "I've told you. He once propositioned me in a very coarse manner, and of course I told him where he could go."

Another woman in answer to the same question, said to *her* husband: "When I turned him down, he hit me."

A third woman took a more liberal view. "Well, dear," she said to her husband, "before I ever knew you existed I fell in love with a couple or three S.O.B.'s. And Steven Masters was one of them. It only lasted three nights with him, so don't be jealous."

The total time she named was correct. What she didn't mention was that, in terms of quantity, three nights with Steven was the equivalent of three months with her husband.

Puzzled wives of males who had been harmed by Steven received replies like: "I told him at one of his parties that he was a spoiled brat. And he had me fired from my job." "I objected to an opinion he volunteered about poor people; so he has an agreement with my publisher to buy up a small first printing of my books, and then he doesn't distribute them. I haven't been read for years, except maybe by Steven. I think he would read them because the better the book the more pleasure he would get out of having it suppressed."

At the door of the auditorium a machine silently examined everyone who entered. Detectives drew three men aside, relieved them of concealed weapons, and then allowed them to enter.

Steven, when he was informed, thought that a surprisingly small number of outright ill-wishers. Glencairn, who addressed the audience in his brisk courtroom manner, did not dwell long on Steven's sins. He did make a brief comment about the trial.

"It was my first military trial," he said, "and I was amazed at the disinterest in actual evidence. Steven was ostensibly tried for not going to Mittend, but he was sentenced for having committed three murders while he was there.

"What Steven wants to do is give every invited person in this room ten thousand dollars. And forgive and forget."

As the figure was mentioned, there was a stirring and a shuffling and a drawing in of breath all over the auditorium. Then, a pause while the audience—at least part of it—multiplied ten thou by nine hundred. Those who could do that in their heads were—and that was the next reaction—audibly impressed.

They began to clap. Doubtful types, or those persons who couldn't multiply, were swept along with the majority. The clapping grew louder and more sustained. It ended when Glencairn held up his hands, and said:

"Anyone who's willing to let bygones be, can go to the back of the room as soon as this meeting is over. We've got thirty girls with certified checks already made out. All you do is sign a simple four-sentence release, in which you agree that you absolve Steven of all blame in your own mind.

"As you can see, it's to your double advantage to really mean it. First of all, it may free you of any future threat of being involved in the kind of unpleasant mind-switch that Mark Broehm and Daniel Utgers are still involved with. And second, of course, is the money. Steven and his father hope you can use that for something special that you've always wanted to do or wanted to buy."

Disappointingly, not everyone went back to pick up the check when the time came. Eighty-one people evidently had just shown up to listen, and the majority of these wished to establish before witnesses that they were among the invited.

Seventy-three of the non-signers at a later date filed suit for damages on a far greater level than ten thousand dollars. There was no evidence of collusion among this group. Each separately, apparently, had the same gleeful thought: What an opportunity to really get some of the Masters money!

Having been invited to Steven's forgive-and-forget fiesta, they would be able to tell their story in court, and it would be difficult for Steven to deny that the injury had taken place. Presumably, he could contest the severity of the harm he had caused, but that would be the limit of his defense.

These intended-to-be-irritating consequences of the meeting took place at a much later date than the plaintiffs intended. The reason was that the government took action. The guests emerged into a night street that literally swarmed with soldiers. Nearby, a long line of buses was drawn up, and into these, protesting and appalled, the members of Steven's audience, the members of Steven's staff, and Stephanie and Glencairn were firmly and, where necessary, forcibly guided.

The elder Masters, since he could not be protected in such a confined space, had thoughtfully stayed away.

CHAPTER 21

★★★★★★★★★★★★★★★★★★★★★★★★★★

The headline the next morning was:

GOVERNMENT ARRESTS THE 1000 NAMES OF STEVEN MASTERS

Under the headline, the story began:

Charging fraud, the administration moved last night to take into custody more than 900 persons and an equal number of accompanying friends or relatives, who attended a so-called forgiveness party on behalf of Steven Masters, the well-known playboy heir to the Masters industrial empire, who is currently languishing in jail.

Confirming the roundup, the Secretary of Defense said, "Our country has been victimized by the spoiled brat of a well-to-do family. All persons who assisted in the hoax will be tried in the courts and fined or jailed as a lesson to anyone else who has in mind treating the sincere and brave efforts of the armed forces with contempt and disdain."

The news story went on to state that all the arrested individuals were taken to New York military headquarters, and screened. As a result they were divided into four groups.

The first group, easily identified, consisted of the detective agency, which had been employed by Masters, Senior, to supervise the entire operation. The agency's permanent and temporary staffs were separated from the guests and released by about three A.M., and with them, attorney Glencairn.

The second group—over 900—were the guests of the so-called harmed persons. They were released shortly before dawn.

The third group—also over 900 people—was, of course, made up of the people Steven Masters claimed to have harmed. The individuals of this third group were turned over to the police. The charges against them, according to the city attorney's office, would be overt participation in a hoax designed to reinforce the numerous falsehoods perpetrated by Steven Masters on the authorities and on a credulous world. All of those persons would eventually be released on bail, but at the request of the military such release was being delayed for several days for security reasons. Trial dates would, of course, be set later.

The fourth "group" was Stephanie.

Stephanie was not turned over to the civil authorities. Instead, she was escorted by six soldiers and a second lieutenant along dimly lighted steel and concrete corridors, and was eventually brought to a halt before a large, heavy steel door. The young lieutenant knocked.

A man's voice, muffled: "What is it?"

"I have the prisoner you wish to question, General Sinter."

"Just a moment."

A pause. Then the clacking of metal against metal. The door swung open silently. The man who stood in the doorway was a complete stranger to Steven insofar as appearance was concerned. But the name and the voice were enemies of nearly two weeks' familiarity.

The face had a faint mocking smile on it. Sinter resembled a middle-aged politician Steven had once met. The same neatness of appearance. Roundish face. Blue eyes. Small brown moustache.

"Well, well," Sinter said heartily, "pretty little lady."

"Not so little," said Steven. As he remembered her, Stephanie at five-feet, five-and-half-inches had always been a fairly good armful. She had, it seemed to him, slimmed down a little since those days, but that was the only difference.

The general stepped out into the corridor, and drew the steel door shut behind him. "To the roof!" he commanded.

They took an elevator, and emerged upon a brightly lighted level landing field—the stereotyped roof kind, with its blast-protected shelters, and all that. A heli-jet stood beside one of the shelters. Its lights were on, and there was a pilot's head visible in the cabin at the front.

"Put her aboard!" ordered Sinter.

Steven had been doing his brand of thinking. Hastily, he said to the young officer and to the men, "I should be accompanied by a woman guard."

The young officer said coolly, "One will be waiting when you land."

"I don't believe that," said Steven in Stephanie's most musical soprano.

Sinter had listened to the interchange with his smile. Now, he stepped in front of the Stephanie body, and said, "Steven, this is your zero hour. You've been escorted up here by seven Gi-Ints. The pilot over there is also a Gi-Int, and of course so am I. These persons who tipped off the newspapers defeated you, because we had no idea of what you were up to until that news account appeared the day of the meeting. Buying off those harmed people was sharp, but we've got them all under lock and key. And, since your own Steven body remains in the control of a Gi-Int named Emmett Obdan, no matter where you switch to you'll find yourself in the same confinement."

He bowed. Straightening, he said, "So, if you will climb aboard, I shall deliver this delectable female body to our leader and father, Kroog."

Steven was interested. "Hey, you're one of Mother's brood on that Gi-Int deal?"

"Yes."

"All those naked people on Mittend—you're one of them?"

"That's where Mother put us when she discovered we had all those unacceptable-to-her qualities," said the general.

Steven said, "My old man and I had you pegged for a colleague of Kroog, because you did that undertone talking—sort of a second personality—when you interviewed me. Mother said the real invaders had difficulty adjusting to this galaxy. Your habit had that look to it, when we thought about it."

"We offspring," said Sinter, "have the same problem. The real Sinter's subconscious thoughts came through. However, there's only one colonist: Kroog. It took everything they had over there to put one life-force across eight hundred thousand light-years."

"Why didn't all the kiddies—your brothers and sisters—come to Earth?"

"What!" Cynically. "And lose contact with Mother?" Sinter did his smile. "You see, Mittend is where she connects to this time universe. So there's no escape for her, Steven. She'll have to give in to Kroog soon for reasons related to all those energy-flows she works with."

The middle-aged man in the uniform of a general frowned at the female who had been talking to him so briskly. "Let *me* ask a question," he said. "You've been unusually calm in all these dangerous situations. Kroog and the others all noticed it. How would you explain that, for a ne'er-do-well?"

"I'm a stupe," Steven said frankly.

"Huh?"

"I can't keep my mind on anything more than a second or two at a time. This conversation keeps going only because you're there, and that keeps reminding me where I am. I've always been like that."

"But, surely, danger—"

"My old defense was stream of consciousness on a

negative association basis. But I seem to have surfaced from that," Steven said cheerfully.

"I must admit," said Sinter, "I'm not happy with this plan of Kroog's. But he's determined to put you under extreme pressure, and then see what you can do to escape."

Steven remembered Obdan. "I thought I was already under extreme pressure," he said. "That's when I became beautiful Stephanie."

"That gave us a clue," was the reply. "So now we're ready for the main event."

"What clue?"

"That you could now switch into the bodies of people whom you helped in some way. So that's where we are now. Climb aboard, please."

There seemed to be nothing else to do. Steven-Stephanie gracefully walked forward, stepped daintily into the low-slung cabin. Sinter followed close behind her. The door swung shut with a faint hissing of air suction.

A minute later the heli-jet was in the air.

CHAPTER 22

****

"The way I see this whole universal-consciousness business," said the voice of Mark Broehm to Captain Odard, "is that it can happen when you follow the rules exactly. So it comes down to mathematics."

They were flying over a particularly wild stretch of Mittend wilderness: mountains, streams, trees, brush. The commanding officer of the craft was intent on the ground below, looking for possible signs of life. As a consequence, it took a minute or so before the gist of what had been said came into him.

It was not the kind of statement that he had come to expect from the Mark Broehm body. So he did a double take on the words, felt suitably blank, but finally he said matter-of-factly: "That bars you from the game, I presume, since your profession as Daniel Utgers is that ancient history thing. However, remember you had the feeling you could locate that girl, and you didn't—so, careful."

"Right now," said the Mark Broehm voice, "I'm Steven Masters again, and I'm here as a result of the stress the Gi-Ints are putting on poor Stephanie Williams. They didn't know that the old man paid off Daniel, and so I had a place to go—up here to replace Daniel."

Captain Odard blinked. He had actually only momentarily looked away from the wilderness. His heart

145

and his spirit, so to speak, were still in communion with the ground beneath the heli-jet.

Steven had time to say, "I'm only up here while I think about those rules as they have been revealing themselves." He added, "Mathematics passed me by, as did a lot of other things. But I have a gut logic, which seems to fit this whole business."

Odard leaned back in his seat. Then he glanced at the pilot. Finally, he looked over at the Mark Broehm body. "Are you telling me," he said in an outraged voice, "that you switched with Dan Utgers and put him in a torture situation while you escaped?"

Steven shook Mark Broehm's head. "It wasn't exactly a torture condition," he said. "When I left, all of Stephanie's clothes had been stripped from her, and General Sinter was just taking off his shorts preparatory to getting into bed with her. It was a psychologically embarrassing moment, so I said, 'Mother—switch me!' And she did it instantly. Boy, that's a relief."

Odard could actually feel his scalp crawl, as he visualized the action that must by this time be getting under way in a little bedroom ten light-years distant. He gulped. If he now saw anything at all of the landscape below it was strictly as a smear of dark green. "Are you telling me—" he screeched, and stopped, startled by the piercing sound of his own voice. He grew aware that Steven-Broehm was staring at him.

A captain of an exploring interstellar expedition is essentially a calm, sane man, not given to extravagances of emotion. But Robert E. Odard could feel the hysteria backing up all the way into his toes, with a tendency to want to squirt out in every direction. "You mean to tell me," he screamed, "that you put that poor history professor into a situation like—"

Once more, he couldn't go on. The blankness descended on his mind again, and finally he just sat there and felt exhausted.

Broehm-Steven said, "No, when you're making test runs, the way I figured it, you might just as well go for broke. So I couldn't see any value in having the, uh, professor in the circuit at all. I told Mother to switch him into his own body. So I imagine that wherever Mark Broehm was with the Utgers body, that body is now heading in the direction of Westchester."

"You mean," mumbled Odard, "Mark Broehm?"

"One of these days," said Steven, "when this universal consciousness, of which Mother seems to be the center, gets us all aware of being connected with each other, I suppose it won't matter who's in that bed, so long as the genital equipment is interlocking."

There was a look of terror on the officer's face, and Steven stopped. The captain swallowed as the meaning of the term made its first impact on his mind.

"Universal consciousness," Odard began. "Isn't that a metaphysical idea that—"

"In those swift early minutes," said Steven, "I had to take it for granted that a girl doesn't mind being a girl. So, though Utgers in this early stage of feeling contact with everybody else couldn't find that wild girl, Mother of course could. So I switched her into Stephanie. She and Sinter are young sister and old brother, considering that there was a span of twenty years while Kroog had Mother under his control. Perhaps, what Mark Broehm observed about the way the women were kept apart will work out between Sinter and Stephanie."

"What favor did you do that wild girl?" asked Odard, who had had his briefing from Earth on that Steven development.

Steven blinked at him. "You're missing the point of universal consciousness," he said. "I, as an individual, can only participate in it according to the rules governing neophytes—the law of the nature of the thing. But where mother can switch, and manipulate, all those others, that is another level of operation. They've been connected a long time. They may not deserve it, but they're her children, and she grants them special rights."

The Mark Broehm face smiled grimly. "And that, my friend, is where the new father—as I suddenly reasoned it in my fashion—can exercise total power. You have to remember," he went on, "that these women came from early Greece. And if you've ever met a modern Greek male, you'll realize that Greece is not where the Women's Lib movement got started."

"Universal consciousness?" Odard started again, tentatively.

"Tell the pilot to veer slightly to the left," commanded Steven.

"Huh!"

"The battle has started up ahead there," was the reply, "and we should, first of all, photograph it. And then, in case some of the women weaken, or get confused, we should participate." He finished, with a frown, "Of course, that still leaves those who are currently visiting Earth. But, still—we can make a start," said Steven.

Odard parted his lips to make something—a sound, a word, a question. It was never spoken.

The pilot had turned. "Hey," he said. "Look up ahead there. Am I dreaming? Somebody's moved the San Diego Zoo to Mittend."

No other words were spoken for a while. Because as far as the eye could see there were monsters: giant snakes, elephants, tigers, great apes, crocodiles, leopards, huge bears. Beasts of Earth. Thousands of them.

Screaming, roaring, snarling, trumpeting, plainly audible as the heli-jet hissed softly over the tangled mass of battling creatures. It turned out later that the cameras caught an entire pack of lions as they attacked two tigers and tore them to bits. Two elephants were photographed stamping a crocodile to death with their feet. And more. Four leopards ripped into a snake thirty feet long, and with fangs that never stopped slashing, darted in and out, avoiding the snake's desperate effort to envelop them or strike one or another with its writhing head.

Suddenly, the Gi-Int must have realized that the stupid peace-lovers meant it.

Whole groups of monsters began to disengage. They

ran. They clawed. They fought now with the total intent of escaping.

Suddenly, one of the fleeing beasts was a hundred feet ahead of its pursuers. There was a rapid blurring effect. Steven was amazed to feel his eyes twist. . . . At *this* distance, he thought.

He had no time to consider it. When he could see again, a leopard had transformed into an eagle, which launched itself awkwardly into the sir, gained speed, and began to fly strongly.

A mere minute after that, there were a score of the huge birds, then a hundred, and finally many hundred. All beating the air with their powerful wings.

Too late, they saw the heli-jet. It came at them, bristling with machine guns, all of them blazing away. For a while the sky rained feathers and dead eagles. Yet as the aircraft came out of its dive, and began to turn, at least a thousand eagles were now flying east.

None of them could possibly fly as fast as the gleaming demon of metal with its colossal armament. Everywhere, eagles plummeted and feathers fluttered.

The survivors evidently had a thought, for they now cunningly tried to turn toward the mountains to the north.

Under Steven's direction, the heli-jet flew over the surface of Mittend, and located, one after the other, the various bands of Gi-Ints as each, in turn, was attacked. Stubbornly, the crew mowed down survivors of the ground battle who tried to escape by air.

It was not impossible, they admitted afterward, that an eagle, or two, or three, got away. The creatures had separated and darted in every direction, including up. And there were, unfortunately, a few clouds.

"Besides," said Steven, "as I thought, some of those Mothers got confused. I have to hand it to the majority, though. They finally, when I insisted, took a correct look at their misbegotten brood, and allowed them to be killed."

"But—but—" said Odard. "There were thousands of kids. Where did all those types come from who killed them?"

"Mother, herself."

"Mother is only 886 people, presumably capable of being elephants and tigers. I'll swear that we participated in a dozen or so battles, and that the total came to at least forty thousand beasts attacking about sixteen or seventeen thousand. By the time we got in there, they were pretty well decimated."

Steven, who was sitting in one of the front seats, spread his hands. "Listen," he said. "In the final issue Mother's problem is not quantity. Mother is everybody."

"That's what you keep saying."

"That's the whole point of universal consciousness," said Steven. "Total connection with every living being. I thought I explained it to you, earlier."

"Yeah, I guess you did," Odard said glumly.

CHAPTER 23

★★★★★★★★★★★★★★★★★★★★★★★★★★

When you sit at the apex of an industrial empire, as Steven Masters, Senior, had done since age 24½ (when his own father had died in a jet crash), you have a better-than-average view of the world.

In these, his middle years, the great man (which is what he had turned out to be—just holding two billion dollars steady was a feat of surpassing skill) always, still, walked quickly. Was interested. Listened. Stayed on the job. And pretty well acted all the time as if he knew what he was doing.

He had a continuing throat problem that just about drove his son batty. Yet an automatic speech slowdown method had survival value. It gave you time to think so you could say no instead of yes.

By noon of the day after the mass arrests, Glencairn, acting on Masters' direction, had assumed the defense of those accused persons who were without counsel. As a consequence he was demanding from the city attorney the location of one Stephanie Williams, who had received payment of $10,000 but could not be found among the persons still detained.

A hopeful deputy city attorney, visualizing prospects for quicker advancement, put a call through to the district military command, and got a "we'll-check" reply. It all seemed very routine to the genuine human beings involved.

It seemed that the military was having its own problems. A Sergeant Obdan in the prison section had suddenly disappeared. Literally vanished into thin air in front of armed guards. What confused the issue was that a large snake had to be exterminated before the search for the missing man could be properly initiated.

What about Steven Masters? Well, keep this quiet, but he was in the psychiatric ward under observation because he had suddenly burst into tears and screamed that he was a girl named—named—

"Damn it!" said the informant. "I don't have the girl's name noted down. But it doesn't matter. That was several days ago, and he's changed his story. He's now Mark Broehm again. At the time, one of the guards called a doctor before Obdan, who was on duty and has recently become quite a disciplinarian (I hear), could stop him."

When that information was passed along, Masters, Senior, said quietly, "We'd like the name of the guard who called that doctor."

Afterward, he mused: So Steven is back on Mittend. . . .

He decided hastily that was not information to pass on to his wife. He had previously reassured her by pointing out that at least while Steven was in jail, "we know where he is."

The Masters industrial complex subscribed to, among many other services, a worldwide interlocking computer network. Into *that,* a Masters troubleshooting engineer inserted a program based on careful instructions from the super-boss. A little later, said engineer placed a list of over 1,900 names on Masters' desk. The names were arranged alphabetically, so it took only a minute for Masters to glance at a few samples, and to notice that there was . . . Patrick Sinter, and Emmett Obdan, and Vint Kroog.

His gray eyes glistened as he scanned the pages and pages of names and addresses. But he said nothing.

The engineer, who had been standing, waiting, expressed his puzzlement: "I don't really understand your criteria, sir. How would anyone ever suspect that the Secretary of Defense is connected to the peculiar requirement you put in about a mistress or female relative being found dead and partly eaten?"

The man shook his head. "The names of the girlfriends of famous men," he said, "are a part of that section of the computer's programming which is normally available only to two government agencies, and that by a special code system. But of course if you say give me the names of women who have been killed and partly devoured, *that* is available. And if you look her up, you discover that under *her* name is all the rest of the information."

"Sir," the engineer finished with a frown, "there're an awful lot of partly eaten female bodies out there—for a civilized world. What do you make of it?"

"One minute!" said the great man. "I'd like you to step into the outer office. I've just realized I must make a phone call."

The call was to a man in India. His swarthy face came onto the viewplate. The entire conversation was in code.

The meaning of Masters' first sentence was: "Are you still in the assassin business?"

"We do that, you who once turned me down totally."

"How many agents do you have available?"

"Enough."

"Nineteen hundred?"

"Yes."

"Could you have a back-up man, also, just in case?"

"Yes."

"I have a list. Get your copying machine?"

"We'll do that."

The list was duly transmitted over another line. The subsequent discussion of the funding of the project was also in code. Then: "When?" said Masters.

"Yes."

Which meant today or tomorrow at the latest.

"Now, one more thing," began Masters.

A pause . . . that grew long.

The Hindu finally spoke a code word that meant: get-on-with-it-sir.

The billionaire gulped. "Can your people get inside a military prison?"

"We'll do that later."

"Less than a—?" The code for week.

The reply was yes.

"My son, Steven Masters, Junior," said Steven Masters, Senior, "is in—" He named the location.

This time the pause came from the other end of the connection. The swarthy face acquired a mottling look of shock. After many seconds, the assassin chieftain said, "We, here in India, are family people. It is difficult for us to conceive of a father who—"

"Life is very strange," acknowledged Steven's father. "There can come a moment when a parent has to recognize that his offspring is a disaster—which could be tolerated so long as his activities were only dimly known to the public."

The grim face on the viewplate grew thoughtful. Finally: "We'll do that."

The face faded. The machine fell silent. Masters realized that he was trembling for the first time in many a long year.

I, he thought, am either insane to believe in what I'm doing. Or else I'm just about to save Earth.

It was not exactly clear from what. But as usual he had followed through every logical sequence.

CHAPTER 24

★★★★★★★★★★★★★★★★★★★★★★★★★★★

How dull can things get?

Try the psychiatric ward of a military prison. A few groaners—but that repetition gets damned tiresome, meaning dull. But mostly the patients are silent and look unconscious. Among both groups are the real far gone, and a few shirkers.

To rate continued special treatment plus abatement of hard labor, the shirkers usually try extremes: extra groaning or extra near-deathness.

There was, of course, an exception. In the bed at the rear of Ward 13, Steven was sitting up. He had already cajoled a magazine from a nurse, and he was reading some schlock. Which was better than nothing-to-do-but-sit-or-lie.

The psychiatrist came through the door, stopped, and looked over at Steven. Then he walked over. "Well, Mr. Masters," he said dryly, "feeling better, I see."

Steven looked back at him with slightly narrowed eyes. Then he tossed the blankets aside. But he continued to sit up, except that perhaps his legs drew in a little more tightly against his bottom.

He said softly, "I sense you're going to make one last effort, Kroog."

"It occurred to me," said the man who looked exactly like Thomas Painter, M.D., psychiatrist, "that a medical doctor is like a god in this Earth society."

"True," Steven acknowledged warily.

"Particularly here in a military prison," said Kroog. "I brought along some equipment. Can you tell me at this penultimate hour why I shouldn't use it?"

"You've got enough to kill?" asked Steven.

Kroog nodded.

"One instant," said Steven, "before you squeezed the trigger, or whatever it is you have to do, you would fall dead. Mother is solidly lined up to protect me."

"They can't kill," said Kroog. "It's genetically imposssible."

"They *have* killed. It's psychologically possible."

"I don't really understand," said Kroog in a plaintive voice, "how you figured that out."

"It's very simple. Ordinary people are not killers on their own. But when a proper authority tells them what to do, they do it. I was the proper authority—the ancient Greek husband-military commander-king."

He let that penetrate, then said: "Remember, Kroog, we're now talking"—earnestly—"about the fate of the original you."

"And the original you," said Kroog.

"Everyone else wanted to kill you, along with all those others." Steven spoke slowly. "I said, 'Kroog is our only contact with another galaxy.' I said I thought somebody—not me, because that's not my style—ought to think a long time before we did a final thing like death. However"—he made a shrugging movement with his hunched-up body—"if we let you live, we have to have you where you can't escape easily, and where I can talk to you for a minute every day through Mother. So—"

Steven braced himself. "That's why, Kroog. You'll be questioned many times. There must be a reason why you adjusted so badly to this galaxy. So aggressively."

"Look who's talking," said Kroog.

And jumped.

Steven rolled with the first crash of the other's body against his. Simultaneously, he grabbed with both hands. With his right, he snatched at the doctor's jacket worn by the other man. He ripped it from top to bottom. With his left hand, he caught at the trousers. It almost seemed, then, as if Kroog's clothes were made of paper, or else had been carefully readied for swift disassembling (that last was the truth), for they came apart, and off.

But Kroog had him now, also. With equal ferocity he tore the pants of Steven's pajamas.

Tugging and twisting and tearing at each other, the two bodies, with bare skin beginning to show, fell off the other side of the bed, out of sight.

How exciting can things get?

Try a psychiatric ward when a patient attacks a doctor. Naturally, that was the conclusion drawn by all observers. With four exceptions, the other patients in the ward were severely stimulated.

The exceptions lay, unmoving, blank, like dead. The demonstrative ones, of course, did their variations of reaction. What counted was that some of them set up a howling sound.

At which attendants started to come in like shots out of a slow gun. But fast enough.

It turned out that the principal job they had was grabbing at and separating two very similar bodies, one of which had a lot of blood on his face, which seemed at the beginning only to be half there.

"Get me a towel!" the doctor mumbled, holding his hands over his mouth and face.

They brought him a towel. Then they brought him bandages. Then somebody came with a couple of robes.

The Steven body was thereupon led off to solitary confinement. The doctor, after asking for his torn clothes—which he said contained his keys and his billfold—and after asking that he be led to his car, mumbled through his bandages, "I'll be all right."

Approximately ten minutes later Steven considered it safe to remove the bandages. It took a little longer to peel off the face mask, which they had got on somewhat crooked to begin with, but which in a twisted fashion did resemble Dr. Painter. The torn clothes contained a chemical solution that presently did a pretty clean job for him.

Steven took a ferry over to New Jersey, and then drove to a farmhouse an hour's driving distance from Patterson, Pennsylvania. It had been midafternoon when he started. It was dark when he got there.

That night, shortly after one A.M., the roof of the barn folded open and a stubby jetlike craft lifted up into a cloud sky. Its passage through the air created a hissing, rustling sound. But that faded. Then the barn folded back into being a barn again.

And there was left the stillness of rural Pennsylvania. . . .

"Hey!" said Steven.

Bright-eyed, he stared down at a shining city. New. Gardenlike. From this height he could see the stream that went through the center of the gleaming stone and marble spread of buildings.

It was only in the final minute before his craft landed that he suddenly realized that what he was seeing wasn't actually a city at all.

It was an estate, with thousands of buildings, large and small. But they were residential structures.

He came down beside the stream, just about where he had first seen the crocodile.

Everything looked sensationally different. The perfect newness of what he could see, compared to the ruins he remembered, was startling.

Steven stepped onto the grassy sward from his ship, drew a deep breath of Mittendian air, and then walked toward the nearest building. It was a residence, and had something of old Greek design in it. Perhaps it was the palace of a minor king. Or queen.

A pathway through a stately garden brought him swiftly to the imposing marble entrance. A female servant opened the door for him, and led him to a large room, with high, bright, stained-glass windows. There was a woman in the room. She looked young and pretty of face, and wore a fluffy white gown. She had been sitting, reading. Now, she put the book aside, stood up, and smiled at Steven.

Steven walked over to a settee near her. "Which one are you?"—he said.

"Ritu."

Steven settled down onto the settee, and put his feet on a small statue within leg reach. "Well, kid," he said, "tell the girls Pop is here."

"They know." The smile was suddenly more tentative. . . . Was it possible that there was already in her manner a hint of a Steven female anxiety? "Is there anything I can get you, Steven?" she asked earnestly.

"I stay with you about eight hours—right?"

Ritu nodded tensely, expectantly.

"Well"—Steven shrugged—"then we've got plenty of time to get acquainted. So, since I'm a little tired, why don't I take a short nap?"

He settled himself lengthwise on the settee. "Wake me in about ninety minutes. The biofeedback people tell me that's one complete sleep-cycle. See you?"

He fell asleep almost immediately.